NOBODY'S BABY

BOOKS BY OLIVIA WAITE

DOROTHY GENTLEMAN

Murder by Memory
Nobody's Baby

FEMININE PURSUITS

The Lady's Guide to Celestial Mechanics
The Care and Feeding of Waspish Widows
The Hellion's Waltz

NOBODY'S BABY

OLIVIA WAITE

Tor Publishing Group
New York

This is a work of fiction. All of the names, characters, organizations, places, and events portrayed in this work are either products of the author's imagination or used fictitiously.

NOBODY'S BABY

Copyright © 2026 by Olivia Waite

All rights reserved.

Interior art © Adobe Stock

A Tordotcom Book
Published by Tom Doherty Associates / Tor Publishing Group
120 Broadway
New York, NY 10271

www.torpublishinggroup.com

Tor® is a registered trademark of Macmillan Publishing Group, LLC.

EU Representative: Macmillan Publishers Ireland Ltd, 1st Floor, The Liffey Trust Centre, 117–126 Sheriff Street Upper, Dublin 1, D01 YC43

The Library of Congress Cataloging-in-Publication
Data is available upon request.

ISBN 978-1-250-34226-3 (hardcover)
ISBN 978-1-250-34227-0 (ebook)

The publisher of this book does not authorize the use or reproduction of any part of this book in any manner for the purpose of training artificial intelligence technologies or systems. The publisher of this book expressly reserves this book from the Text and Data Mining exception in accordance with Article 4(3) of the European Union Digital Single Market Directive 2019/790.

Our books may be purchased in bulk for specialty retail/wholesale, literacy, corporate/premium, educational, and subscription box use. Please contact MacmillanSpecialMarkets@macmillan.com.

First Edition: 2026

Printed in the United States of America

10 9 8 7 6 5 4 3 2 1

TO EVERY STRANGE BABY WHO EVER SMILED AT ME IN REAL LIFE—KEEP BEING GLORIOUS LITTLE MONSTERS, ALL OF YOU

THE NOTE FROM Ruthie arrived at breakfast with no preamble, flashing on the glowing face of my pocket watch: *At what age do human children grow teeth?*

On the long list of things my nephew didn't know, this was one of the least surprising. His expertise was deep but mostly limited to three topics: operation scripts for the sentient shipmind, cocktail combinations, and his husband, John.

Even back on Old Earth, three and a half centuries before, I doubted he had spent much time around children. I hadn't, either—Ruthie himself being the exception—but I wasn't about to admit it.

A quick search through the ship's infobank got me the answer to his question: *six months to a year*. I sent it along, then sat back with a restorative sip of tea.

True peace proved elusive: Unease flowed in with the bergamot in my breakfast blend.

The little light on my pocket watch's case flickered, indicating my nephew had replied. I opened it and glanced down. *And what age do they start speaking?*

Twelve to eighteen months, I sent back, after more research.

I finished my tea.

After a long moment, and slowly, as if each letter were being inked in my own heart's blood and I had to wait for it to ooze out drop by drop, I followed up: *. . . Why?*

A small silhouette of clock hands spinning, the sign Ruthie was composing a reply. I rose from the table to put my teacup in the washer, the better to give myself one final moment of respite.

His response: *Then I fear the poor thing will be able to bite us before they can explain why they're so upset.*

This was one of those times I hated being right.

I rubbed the burgeoning headache from my temples. Unbelievable. Here we were, in a spaceship endless light-years from Earth, on the way to a home we'd never seen, with ten thousand adults whose bodies had been carefully treated to prevent conception and reproduction so the population would remain stable for the length of our centuries-long journey across the stars—

—and Ruthie had somehow managed to come up with a baby.

And of course, as a ship's detective, and Ruthie's only relative, it was my duty and my thankless task to find out how.

It couldn't be the retromats: Although theoretically they could fabricate anything a person could remember, in practice there were limits on their use. Candles, for instance, were prohibited, because the combination of a spaceship and a naked flame had never led to anything good in all of human history. Living things were also forbidden—though some of the geniuses down in Forward Starboard Seven had managed to make mechanical animals and automata quite persuasively lifelike, using retromatted components. Perhaps this baby was something like that, and Ruthie had only been fooled?

No. Whatever my nephew's faults—and they were legion—he was brilliant with mechanical things. If this alleged baby had been an automaton he'd have written with jubilant delight, not those hurried, harried questions.

But even assuming someone had removed the controls and managed to get a retromat to recreate a living, breathing, apparently screaming human child—the amount of mental focus and energy that implied was astonishing. Implausible. One might even say impossible.

Which left only one other, only slightly less impossible possibility: Someone had made a baby the old-fashioned way. Two human bodies, gooey bits out, overlapping in space and time.

Stars, what a nightmare.

None of us was supposed to be able to bear children during the long passage on the *Fairweather*. The physical rigors of the process were bad enough on a planet, let alone here in the mystery and depths of distant space. Who knew what kind of risks pregnancy would have out here, with the strange magnetics and the physics and the constant threat of radiation? And the birth was only the first step! After that you had to educate them, to help them grow and thrive, and while we weren't ever going to run out of food or water or cocktail supplies, this was a ship, and living space was our most finite resource.

It was thought by the architects of our journey that it would be simpler, on the whole, if we simply paused the whole process until we were established on solid ground again.

There was also something... uncanny, let's be honest, about the idea of a human who'd never set foot on solid ground. To have never smelled the rain, felt the sun, dug fingers into the grit and grime of a planet.

Well, now we had one. A child of the stars, born between worlds.

My peace would probably be nonexistent for the next little while.

On my way, I sent to Ruthie.

Then I tucked my watch back in my pocket, wrapped my fern shawl around my shoulders, and set out.

Spring on most of the *Fairweather* wasn't quite the same as spring on Earth. There was no sense of thawing in the air, no change in temperature to signal the flow from one season into another. We counted the months to pass the time. But in the garden of the Greenway, every growing thing seemed to be breathing in after the long winter's exhale: plants poking up from the earth, petals unfurling, leaf buds veiling the once-bare limbs of deciduous trees. A few stray apple blossoms had even woken early, blinking at the humans passing by. I walked through their dappled shadows and caught a hint of that familiar scent, so full of ancient promise, as I made my way down to Ruthie and John's apartment in Forward Port Five.

Nobody answered my knock, but I hadn't expected them to. So I passed my thumb over the lock and let myself in with my detective's access. "Hullo, John," I said, then froze.

For John Pengelly, Ruthie's husband and the most talented mixer of memories on board the *Fairweather*, looked as though someone had tied a rope to his ankle and then dragged him up a set of stairs carpeted in burlap. His stick-straight hair stuck straight in all directions. His eyes rolled white with barely abated panic. His tie had a full inch between the knot and his collar, and his shirt buttons—buttons, plural!—were buttoned wrong. One of them wasn't even buttoned at all!

I couldn't have been more shocked if I'd walked into the room and seen him brandishing a bloody knife over a murdered corpse. Or wearing navy shoes with black trousers.

The hardest part of being a ship's detective was having to see people at the nadir of what they could bear. And John had clearly reached that point.

He was sitting in the center of the floor, surrounded by various lengths of wood. Two of them were clutched in splinter-wracked hands. One lay snapped to one side, beside a metal spring frame with several springs gone sproing.

John looked up at me with haunted eyes. "Dorothy, what are you doing here?"

"Ruthie sent me a note," I replied. I nudged a spar aside with one toe, thinking ominously of shipwrecks. "Where is my dear nephew?"

"Upstairs," John said, and shuddered. "With that creature."

And so thus warned, I ascended to the bedrooms on the second floor.

I could hear the child even before I raised my hand to knock. It was that awful, colicky wail, the kind that went through you like a drill until you fell to pieces. I pushed open the door to the bedroom.

The large bed was as disheveled and exhausted as a feckless youth on day five of a lost weekend. Striding back and forth beside it, bare feet tangling in the coverlet and kicking it aside by turns, was Ruthie: brown curls mussed, sweater sleeves rolled up, bags beneath his eyes, and with—yes indeed—a baby in his arms. He was bouncing it, up and down, as he walked, back and forth, making soothing little shushing sounds in a hopeful voice.

I couldn't resist a fond auntly smile—no matter that my body was currently midtwenties, and Ruthie a good decade older than that. Nephews were nephews, no matter the age.

Ruthie looked up and seized on me, the way a sailor washed overboard seizes the life buoy bobbing by in the maelstrom. "Finally!" he cried, though it had been, at most, ten minutes since my note. "Take this for a moment, will you? I have to see about John."

And he deposited the squalling bundle in my arms and left the room.

The baby wailed harder.

I took a deep and bracing breath.

If I was going to solve the mystery of where this baby had come from, I was first going to have to solve the mystery of how to get them to shut their adorable trap. And fast, before the three of us lost our minds.

The baby wailed again. I ignored that for the moment and looked the infant over. They were young, quite young.

No teeth, as my nephew had noticed, and young enough to be colicky. They had a pinafore-type garment wrapped around them, and beneath that—fortunately—was a diaper that—fortunately—was fresh and properly applied to their—likely *his*—anatomy. So that was one problem we weren't having yet.

Oh, sweet stars, we were going to have to toilet train him at some point, weren't we?

My arms must have tensed, or else the baby didn't like that thought any more than I did. The wails increased.

I had one other card to play. Most of my memories of Earth were faded things by now, fragile and weathered as album photographs. But some moments stayed shining. My first kiss in a London sunrise. The smell of the sea on a summer afternoon when I was eight. And the first time I'd met Ruthie, when after two weeks of a miserable ocean crossing, I walked into my sister's New York brownstone and she'd put a tiny, burbling little human being into my arms.

I went back down the stairs and stepped into the middle of an argument. Ruthie and John both went silent as I appeared, identical looks of dread painted over their faces.

I ignored them to walk to the kitchen, the babe's persistent cries trailing behind me like a scarf.

The retromat had no trouble producing a bottle just like the one I'd used all those hundreds of years ago. The nipple popped into the open mouth, the lips snapped shut, and then—blissful silence. The thoughtful sucking noises barely even qualified as sounds, in comparison.

The baby stared up at me, his eyes full of wonder as he slurped down the memory of a meal from three centuries before.

"Hello there," I whispered, smiling back.

I swayed gently back and forth, mostly for something to do, and after a long minute Ruthie appeared at my side. "Oh," he whispered, hardly more than a breath. "Oh, Aunt Dorothy, you saint. You miracle worker."

I pursed my lips. "He was hungry, that's all," I said, not whispering, though I kept my tones low and soothing. "I'll fill your icebox before I leave here. You can take over with your own memories after that."

"How in the stars did you do that?" John rasped. Ruthie shushed a warning, but it was hardly needed: John's voice sounded as worn out as though every scream of the baby's had been scraped from his own vocal cords. And then his eyes sharpened, some of his usual keenness coming back. "How long will it last?"

"Not too long, I fear," I said. "They cry when they're hungry, they cry when they need changing, they cry when they're confused—and they're always confused. They've got no memories, you see—only experiences. Everything is brand-new, unfamiliar, all the sharp edges unblunted." I crooned at the small bundle in my arms. "Who wouldn't cry?"

John visibly gathered himself. "It's fine when he's quiet," he said. "I'm not afraid of the mess. It's only—the noise," he said, and shuddered.

Ruthie patted him consolingly on the shoulder.

John took heart from that and pulled a deep breath into his lungs. "Here," he said, and took the baby and the bottle from me. Settling back into an armchair, he absently pulled a cashmere blanket down from the back and wrapped it around the infant, who was now looking as blissful and serene as a cat in a patch of sunlight.

It wouldn't last, and I knew it, but still my heart caught at the sight. Just so does the youth ever make fools of their elders. "So," I said, and turned my gaze upon my benighted nephew. "Tell me how it happened."

"Well," Ruthie said faintly. "*Well*. Since you asked." He coughed, and went red, and coughed again, and looked helplessly at John. "Sometimes, when two people—"

"Not babies in general," I interjected, flat horror grabbing me by the throat. "This baby in particular. How did he come to be"—I waved around at the thoughtful decor and precisely placed furnishings of the living room, but also at our great ship and all the universe around it—"here?"

"Oh," Ruthie breathed, relief swirling around him like fog around a particularly dim lamppost. Then he brightened. "Aunt Dorothy, it was just like the flickers! A baby in a basket!"

"There was," John confirmed, "a basket."

"And crying!"

"And," John said darkly, with unplumbed depths of venom, "crying."

"I don't suppose there was a bit of unusual fabric the baby was swaddled in?" I groused. "Some piece of jewelry with a mysterious crest or set of initials?" Mysterious babies were an absolute cliché in the movies and stage plays down on Aft Port Eleven, particularly the nostalgic kind set back on Earth. The baby would turn out to be Lord Such-and-Such's lost heir, and conveniently festooned with clues to the child's origin and proper thread in the social fabric. They were always miracles, plot-wise: repairing sundered family relationships, letting two idiots confess a long-hidden love, generally knitting severed social ties back together seamlessly.

It was too much to expect from a person who couldn't even form comprehensible words yet.

"There was nothing in the basket but the baby," Ruthie said, slumping back. "I'm as disappointed as you are!"

Ruthie could never be as disappointed as I was. He hadn't the constitution.

Even now, he was gazing down at the infant with an expression of pure besotment. "Our first baby," he sighed.

John's eyebrows quirked in alarm. "A little premature, don't you think?"

"By many hundreds of years," I said dryly. "Where was this basket found?"

Ruthie grinned. "On the doorstep, of course. Someone rang the bell two nights ago, just after dinner, and when we opened the door, there was the basket." He blinked. "I say, you don't think the *baby*—"

"No, Ruthie, I don't think the baby rang the bell." I considered. "Do you think the baby was left for you? Or for John?"

John's eyebrows shot up as high as eyebrows could go without rocketing straight off his face. "Me? Why me?" he squeaked.

"Why Ruthie?"

"A fair point," he conceded. The baby murmured, and John's gaze narrowed. "But most importantly: How do we give him *back*?"

"I'm not sure they want the baby back. In fact, I'm fairly certain they don't."

My nephew sucked in a breath. "Why wouldn't they want him?" Ruthie said, the same way he'd have said, *Why wouldn't they want* me?

"If they wanted the baby," I countered, "they'd hardly have left them on your doorstep, would they?" I tapped my fingers. "They could have left him in the Greenway, too—someone would have found him there within a few minutes."

"Especially once he started making noise," John muttered.

"So those are our initial questions," I went on. "One, who left the baby, and two, who are the parents?"

Ruthie's brow scrunched. "Aren't those the same question?"

"Maybe—maybe not. And three . . ." I braced myself. "Is this baby the only one, or are there more?"

John blanched like a whale that has just felt the first harpoon. "Surely not."

I rose from my seat and reached for my coat. "We'll just have to take it one baby at a time. And we start by taking the baby to the Bureau."

John looked grim, Ruthie looked thrilled, and the baby—well, the baby spit up all over John's cashmere blanket.

FOR DISCRETION'S SAKE, we put the baby back into the basket while we took the lift upward to Deck Four: Ruthie with the child, John with a bag of supplies, and me with too many misgivings.

On Four there was no Greenway of light and leaves dividing the ship into port and starboard, just row after row of long businesslike corridors in soft grays and faceted glass. The floors were dark retromatted wood, sturdy and scuffed from three hundred years of hurrying feet. And up here, on the aft side of a small quad with a few benches and one lone red maple beneath a tiny solar lamp, was the two-story space that housed the Detectives' Bureau, where my colleagues and I worked perpetually to untangle the twisted web of human crime, malfeasance, and deceit.

"The Bureau!" Ruthie whispered in awe, clutching the

baby basket to his chest. John's glance at him was fondly exasperated.

I rolled my eyes. My nephew spent his days elbow-deep in ten thousand people's glittering memories, or writing complex chains of logic and thought for a mind the size of a small city—and he was impressed by the place where half a dozen nosy people did the majority of their paperwork and made a little coffee to stave off terminal tedium.

No accounting for taste, I suppose.

Ruthie was all aquiver as I led the way into the waiting room on the ground floor, plush with ochre sofas and innocuous magazines and, luckily for me, empty of people waiting. Normally I'd have stopped him here—but normally he wasn't carrying anything we needed to keep secret. "I'll just take the basket, if you like," I said casually, reaching out for the handle.

Ruthie pulled it out of my reach, causing the baby to give a gurgle of protest and John to go waxen with alarm. "Oh no," my nephew said with all the determination of a horse that's got the bit and wants to gallop, and there's nothing a mere human can do to stop it. "If the baby's going in, I'm coming, too."

I groused, but I yielded. "Very well—but I warn you, Rutherford Talmadge, you've built it up so much in your head it'll never compare to what you've envisioned."

"We'll see about that," he insisted.

I groused a little more, just to make my objections felt, and then led our little troupe up the stairs at the back. I tried valiantly to ignore the small, awed intake of breath from my nephew behind me.

Yes, there were our detectives' offices, all six of them, doors and everything: two glass boxes each on three sides of the upper story. There was the unrestricted retromat, and the infobank with access to databases most civilians would never see the inside of, and a long sturdy research table between them. And there was the kitchenette, in a small frame in the center of the main space, with its icebox and autochef and a sink a single person wide.

Ruthie wouldn't know how to read the centuries' accumulated memories the way a ship's detective could. The way I did.

There was the gash in the floor where Baxenden had tackled a very small man with a very large knife seventy-five years ago; a persistent stain on the counter where some kind of acid had eaten into the tile barely one decade into our journey. The plants in the corners, which Ogilvy babied with distilled water and nitrogenous elixirs and eggshells mixed with coffee grounds—but only when he was stuck on some particularly difficult case. And the glass in Leloup's office, the inside surface of which was half covered in tiny slips of paper carefully taped at right angles to one another—he moved them around constantly as clues blossomed and theories coalesced, but the angles always stayed exact and the space between slips was always one precise centimeter, no more and no less.

And a glimpse of my own office: a much-scarred desk, a squeaky chair in need of reupholstering, a small sofa with a divot made by three hundred years' worth of sitting, and a pile of old books stacked up in the corner of one arm.

The Bureau wasn't just a room to me, it was home. I'd spent more of my waking life here than I had in any of the various apartments I'd lived in on board the *Fairweather*—or even on Earth, before Embarkation. My memories might have been mostly stored in the Library three decks above, but their duplicates haunted this room like friendly familial ghosts.

My nephew held the baby basket up and whispered, "Remember this, little one. Your first time at the Detectives' Bureau."

"Babies that small can't form memories," I reminded him.

The baby made a small chirrup, reminding me in turn that I had a job to do.

Fellow detective Meherbai Petit, in close-tailored tweed, was at the kitchenette's abbreviated counter measuring spiced powder into a carafe. She looked up and smiled, creases lining her warm brown skin at the corners of her eyes. "Hullo, Dot," she said. "Fancy a cup?"

"Love one," I said. Coffee or tea or espresso or chai, it didn't matter: Everything Meherbai brewed was delicious—and could jolt the dead into wakefulness. She did for caffeinated beverages what Monet had done for water lilies.

She cocked her head, brown eyes glinting with interest. "And something for the baby?"

Behind me, Ruthie gave a muffled gasp. "How did she know?" he whispered.

Since the child was currently waving its precious little fists around in the open air above the rim of the basket, it wasn't a particularly staggering leap of logic on Meherbai's part.

"What else can you tell us?" Ruthie demanded, delighted.

Meherbai set the milk to heating and raised a brow at me.

I shrugged and waved: *Please yourself.*

The other detective stepped forward and bent over the basket, her short dark waves falling over her temples. The baby made the sounds babies make when faces come into view. His fist curled around one long brown finger when Meherbai held out a hand.

The detective smiled, her smoky voice amused. "Well, it's a human. Brand-new—four months, maybe? Five?" She waggled her finger, moving the tiny pale fist that clenched tight around it. "Someone's taken good care of you, that's certain."

"You think so?" Ruthie asked.

"Unless you made the basket and the clothes?" My nephew shook his head. "Then yes—those are old patterns, and well remembered. Things someone hasn't had cause to think about in hundreds of years, but they came out perfectly. Or imperfectly, which is much harder to do. Look at the variation in the basket weave, and the lace on the cloth."

"Why abandon a baby they cared about?" John asked.

"Let's go ask them," I replied. I'd taken the opportunity to sidle up to the infobank and do a quick search for who might have retromatted those objects in the past few months. Only one home had done both a basket and a piece of fabric of that type: an address on Aft Port Eleven.

"You'd best take your chai to go," Meherbai said, "before—"

"What," said someone with genteel horror, "is *that*?"

I closed my eyes briefly, calling silently for strength. It was always wise to prepare myself before beginning any conversation with Leloup. "Surely you've seen babies before, Aloïs?" I asked, and turned around.

There he was, my cordial nemesis, one irritating inch taller than me. He was currently just past the peak of middle age, with a small mustache, a soft paternal face, and a mind like a mandoline. "I have also seen murderers, madame," he huffed, "but would be equally displeased to find one of them in my office this morning."

"Hang on—this baby hasn't killed anyone," Ruthie said, staunch in the infant's defense.

"Perhaps it has," Leloup returned crisply. "Childbirth is often so dangerous. This child may have been the instrument of one—or more—of its parents' demise. Until you find the mother, you cannot know."

"Perhaps you should interrogate the baby," Meherbai put in, eyes twinkling. I scowled at her for encouraging him.

Too late. "Would that I could!" Leloup said with a sigh, and a finger to his mustache. "But, alas, this baby has no identification number to put at the top of the form—it has not paid for a berth on our fine ship, so it has no home, no bank account, no memory-book, none of the usual methods we use to distinguish one person from another. How can you interrogate a person who does not exist?"

"Oh, if that's all," Ruthie said, "I expect you might as well ask how a person who does not exist could soil his nappies so many times in one day—but this little man seems to have already solved that philosophical conundrum."

Leloup gave my nephew the particular, profound look of consternation only Ruthie could elicit.

My nephew simply smiled, innocent as the dawn.

I was delighted to see Leloup rendered speechless. However, it couldn't last: Best to leave before he found his tongue again to lecture us. "Shall we go see what his mother can tell us?" I asked.

John shook hands farewell with Meherbai, I nodded regally to Leloup and took my chai with one hand and Ruthie's elbow with the other, and the little group of us passed once again through the waiting room and out of the Bureau.

WE TOOK ONE of the janitorial lifts, the better to keep the baby out of sight. Aft Port Eleven had become the *Fairweather*'s equivalent of a theater district: The apartments were spangled with retromatted marquees that danced and dazzled, electric script scrolling out the theater names—I counted three separate Orpheums, or was that Orphea?—while black block letters listed the current offerings for stage and screen: *Dance Your Way Home*, *The Wings of Battle*, *Twilight Souls*, and so on. Posters with images and start times covered the front windows and blocked light, and food carts studded the walkway selling portable edibles: popcorn, samosas, pastilla, and spring rolls with so many dipping sauces it looked like a painter's palette.

We found ourselves at the address we sought in the middle of the morning matinee. THE PALACE, said the glowing blue outlines with gold filigree. On Earth the signs would have been buzzing from the power needed to set them aflame; on the *Fairweather* they were silent, all that brilliance compounded of bioluminescence from sources both marine and mycological.

That silence always felt a little eerie to me—as though some vast, hungry creature were lying in wait and holding its breath.

"Give me a moment to get the lay of the land," I said; Ruthie found a seat on a convenient bench with John standing beside him, blocking anyone's view into the basket.

I thumbed open the door, passed through the curtained antechamber, and found myself in the theater.

Dim as the place was, it was a minute or two before my eyes adjusted enough to make out details. It was roughly the same size and layout as Ruthie's apartment several decks above—but this place's owner had filled the front room with row after row of sofas upholstered in deep red velvet, all angled to face the screen that stretched the length of the right-hand wall. Clearly it was a good picture, to judge by the rapt looks and ardent attention on the faces of the people in the audience. An upright piano near the back wall was being played with well-honed skill by a young woman with light hair.

About half the seats were full, some with solo viewers and others with couples or trios. They swapped treats back and forth and sipped memory liqueurs, heightening the effect of the flickering scenes. The image was silvered and shimmering: A young couple were running from something, her in a tattered evening gown and him in a tux missing a sleeve. The young woman held a baby-shaped bundle in her arms. Frantic, they climbed into a taxicab and sped off as skyscrapers whizzed by in the windows around them.

I had a visceral shock, as I suddenly remembered what it had felt like to ride in an automobile: the leaning around corners, the acceleration and the sense of momentum, the way braking became a weight pressing on you from behind. Technically the *Fairweather* was traveling much faster right now than any motorcar could have managed—but you try telling the body that. My stomach swooped.

Back in the ordinary light of the walkway, I gasped and waited for my dazzled eyes to readjust. It had been a long time since I'd tried the flickers—perhaps they'd gotten more potent in the past few decades. John and Ruthie looked at me with concern. "That was quick," John said, putting a steadying hand on my elbow.

Ruthie peered at the poster in the window. It was a painting of a baby in thick-framed glasses and too-big lab coat. The young couple, also in lab coats, stood over the baby, mugging comedically but tilted toward one another in a way that any longtime viewer could decode as Romantic Entanglements Ahead. "*The Follies of Youth*," he read in a knowing voice.

"You've seen it?"

He nodded eagerly. "What part are they at?" And when I described what I'd seen: "Only about ten more minutes, then," he said. "It's about a professor who invents a youth serum that works so well it turns him back into an infant."

"Shenanigans naturally ensue," John put in.

Ruthie cackled. "They very much do, yes. At the end of the film the professor is restored to his proper age, the young couple have a passionate kiss, and everyone is exactly the same except better."

"Very realistic," I said dryly.

Ruthie *tsk*ed. "Nobody goes to the flickers for real life, Aunt Dorothy."

How he could sound so virtuous about something so frivolous, I'll never know. The mysteries of a nephew, I suppose.

The passionate kiss was, indeed, very passionate, I found when I slipped back in a few minutes later. Someone sighed, the characters vanished, and the audience stood and stretched as the lights came up.

I went looking for the projectionist.

There she was, a slim brunette with bobbed hair sitting in a high director's chair at the back. She was pulling from her head the flat gray skimmer that plucked the images from her mind and cast them out where the rest of us could watch them. Actual film stock was of course wildly impractical on board a spaceship—even worse than the candles—so instead people donned a skimmer, whose long ribbon fed into a lens and a light on the wall, and beamed their memories out for the entertainment of their fellow passengers.

It was not precisely the same technology used for the memory-books in the Library. Skimmers didn't store anything; they merely reflected what the brain beneath was focused on. How had Ruthie described it? Memory-books were architecture: complex three-dimensional plans of the mind, meant to be re-created precisely. Skimmers offered something more like photographs, quick snaps of a single moment from one point of view, a brief slice of conscious thought made visible through light and shadow.

People had started by trying to replicate the movies they'd seen on Earth—Buster Keaton, Louise Brooks, Laurel and Hardy. But even when projectors worked from a script held in their hands, little changes crept in—lines of dialogue sprouted synonyms and paraphrases, hemlines and hat angles shifted—and then at some point someone realized that if you were already projecting a remembered story that had happened to someone else (Laurel, say, or Hardy), then you could probably project a story that had never actually happened at all.

So someone asked: What if Laurel and Hardy had made a picture with Louise Brooks?

That first experiment, the first new film in fifty years, had been a sensation. While retrospectives still happened from time to time—I saw *The Navigator* anytime it was showing—by far the bulk was now people imagining new stories, right in the open where anyone with a ticket could watch. It was an art, really, to dream so persuasively that other people could slip into it. Like building a café out of raindrops and then inviting someone over for tea.

In the Palace, this theater's projectionist was staring quietly but quite intently at the piano player, who had stood from the bench and was now hoovering the carpet to clear away the crumbs, popcorn kernels, and all the detritus of silver-screen dreams. At the end of the row she turned to the brunette with a smile—a smile I'd seen more than once this morning.

She was the model for the leading lady in the film I'd just caught the end of.

She was also our abandoned baby's mother. I'd stake my detective's privileges on it.

I pulled out my pocket watch and sent John and Ruthie a hasty note, then stepped forward.

The blonde was now peering at the skimmer where her friend held it. "Is it still giving you trouble with the night scenes?"

"They keep wanting to turn into daytime."

"I'm sure Norris will know what's wrong."

"Yes," said the projectionist, with a wry twist to her lips, "I'm sure my son will be thrilled to be of help."

"Mrs. Anne Godfrey?" I asked. This address listed two residents.

"That's me," said the brunette, still in the director's chair.

I smiled at the blonde. "Then you must be Miss Flora Tilburn."

"That's right," she said. Her twinkling eye ran down and then up my figure, making Mrs. Godfrey's brow crease.

I smiled lightly at Miss Tilburn. "I think I may have something that belongs to you," I said.

With exquisite timing, John and Ruthie came in the door. The baby had apparently behaved himself long enough, because he began to cry almost as soon as they entered the theater.

I kept my eyes on Miss Tilburn, who was staring at the baby with her mouth hanging open in an attitude of complete surprise that was rather fetching, honestly.

Mrs. Godfrey, however, had hunched herself into a ball, guilt splashing a dull red over her cheeks.

"What is that?" Miss Tilburn asked.

"That, I believe, is your child," I replied.

The baby helpfully cried harder. His grasping hands opened and closed like hungry little starfish.

"Hang on," Ruthie muttered, "I've got something here . . ."

And he pulled from his coat pocket one of the bottles I'd made for him. Thus muffled, the baby resumed feeding. And staring.

His mother was doing the same. "I don't . . ." Either Miss Tilburn was genuinely flummoxed or she was the greatest actress anyone on the *Fairweather* had ever seen. "I'm not . . ." She shook her head, helpless, gazing down as if hypnotized into eyes the exact shape and shade of her own.

I turned to the brunette. "Mrs. Godfrey? Can you clarify?"

The projectionist burst into tears.

After that, it all came out. How despite a century of being roommates, Miss Tilburn had a bout of mild illness and then moved out to her own apartment last year, suddenly and with no explanation. How she'd even stopped coming to Mrs. Godfrey's flickers for a couple of months, when she'd never missed one before. They kept up a frequent correspondence, but Miss Tilburn had staunchly refused to explain her change of address, beyond a vague "need for space."

The roommate might have been puzzled, but to a detective with Old Earth experience all those things were as good as a neon sign flashing *someone's pregnant and trying to hide it*.

Mrs. Godfrey had been distraught at the separation, anxious for her friend, and when Miss Tilburn had let several notes pass entirely unread, the projectionist had tracked down her new apartment and found nobody home—except for one tiny, angry, crying human in an upper bedroom.

"You didn't report this?"

"I tried! I thought he might be Flora," she confessed, a hint of tears in her voice. "We've been showing *The Follies of Youth* for weeks now. And—the baby had her eyes. But our deck head only said, 'Yes, I've seen that flicker, too, pull the other one.' I figured it was some kind of glitch with the bodies. Babies are supposed to be impossible on this ship, aren't they? And everybody knows that Mr. Talmadge is the best scriptwriter on the *Fairweather*. If anyone could fix this glitch, he could."

"So you left him on Mr. Talmadge's doorstep?" I asked.

"Quite right, too," Ruthie said, patting the girl's shoulder and offering her a handkerchief.

Mrs. Godfrey accepted it gratefully, dabbing at her nose. "And then this morning Flora wrote to ask what we were showing today. Like nothing had happened. I assumed the glitch had been corrected, that she was in a proper body again."

"I just got out of Medical," Miss Tilburn put in weakly. "It had been a few months since I updated my memorybook, and I don't remember moving out. I thought I was coming home. Medical said I'd had some kind of stroke and been brought in three days ago."

"Not uncommon, for people who've recently given birth," I said.

She wrapped her arms around herself, as if trying to hold

her body together. "But I haven't! I may have done—in a previous body—but I don't remember! It's like—like it happened to someone else." She gave a shudder.

Mrs. Godfrey raised a hand and reached for her, but let it drop again.

Miss Tilburn, wiping her eyes, didn't seem to notice.

Ah, so it was like that. Poor Mrs. Godfrey. You would think that having been twenty-five several times over would give you some kind of armor against the worst parts—the reckless impulses, the questionable romantic decisions—but the sad truth is, you cannot wisdom your way out of intense emotions if your body has other ideas.

"So while his mother was having a stroke and being decanted into a new body, the baby was all alone for *two whole days*?" Ruthie demanded, appalled.

"I—I don't think so?" Mrs. Godfrey said, her voice horrified. "She— He was sleeping fairly comfortably when I arrived. And he'd been changed recently."

"So who was taking care of him?" Miss Tilburn whispered.

"The father, most likely," I said, and they all turned to stare at me. I shrugged. "Who else?"

"The father . . . Jason Ipcar?" Mrs. Godfrey bit her lip, and looked everywhere but at her friend. "He's a scenario writer—I project his scripts occasionally, and he and Flora have been an item for a while."

"He's likeliest," Miss Tilburn confirmed, looking equally displeased. "He'll be insufferable, if so. I'm supposed to meet him for tea in half an hour."

"You needn't tell him anything yet," I put in. "We'll be confirming the infant's parentage with Medical as soon as possible. No point in saying anything—to anyone—until we know for sure. Especially if there are multiple possibilities." *And especially if someone was trying to keep the baby a secret for nefarious reasons*, I thought, but kept that idea to myself.

"I think I shall find myself with a headache this afternoon," Miss Tilburn muttered.

Mrs. Godfrey looked slightly relieved, and slightly guilty about it.

"Perhaps you would show us this new apartment?" I asked Miss Tilburn.

The girl shook her head. "If it's all the same to you, I'd much rather you go without me," she said. "I don't even remember anything about living there. It's— It may have been where I stayed for a time, but it's not my home." Her eyes stayed fixed on mine, even as Mrs. Godfrey's eyes stayed fixed on her.

I nodded. "Just as you please." Mrs. Godfrey scribbled out the address for us.

Ruthie took a deep breath and squared his shoulders. "Would—would you like to take the baby?"

Miss Tilburn recoiled—slightly but noticeably. "Again, I'd rather not. If you don't mind. It's been—it's been something of a shock."

"And you just out of Medical," I said, putting a hand on Ruthie's arm to restrain him from saying anything else. "There's no rush. I'll let you know as soon as we have anything concrete to share."

And so the baby came with us, and we left his mother behind.

FLORA TILBURN'S SECRET apartment was on Forward Port Six: People here kept mostly to themselves, and the apartment units were particularly famous for soundproofing, a sense of isolation, and smoked-glass panes preventing anyone from catching a glimpse of the interior. Thick rugs on the walkways muffled our footsteps as we approached the door.

If you wanted to hide your personal life, this was the place you went to do it.

And it seemed Flora had. Yes, there were several outfits for the baby here, and in the icebox was food for both infants and adults that was wilted but hadn't yet had time to spoil. A few dresses—all in Flora's size, and only Flora's size—hung in the closet, but no sign of any second adult inhabitant.

I went to check the door lock just as a neighbor in brown wool was walking by. The baby, upstairs, let out a wail.

The neighbor's step slowed, and their eyes briefly met mine.

I glared at them stonily until they dropped their gaze and hurried away.

Intriguingly, the front door lock had been wiped clean of any entry records, which implied that someone with some technical savvy had been trying to cover their tracks. No real surprise there: Flora and her roommate were both neck-deep in the flicker crowds, who were almost as mechanically adept as the automata folks down on Forward Starboard Seven. Anyone who knew their way around the complexity of a skimmer system would have no trouble with a simple lock.

Perhaps Mrs. Godfrey had reset the lock when she came in and found the baby; perhaps someone else had come by in the days since.

Either way, nothing here told us anything about the other part of the baby's parentage. So it was back in the lift, and up to Medical.

There was a public entrance—a lovely one—but we didn't use it. We went in through the back and to the morgue, where bodies were taken when no longer needed so that they could be broken down into their constituent atoms. It was kept strictly separate from the object-reclamation center down on Deck Seventeen, but the process was essentially the same. There was always a faint but unsettling smell of luncheon meat, whose source the technicians staunchly refused to identify.

"Ferry," I said when we were safely ensconced in the mortician's borrowed office, "I'm afraid I have to ask you about someone's genetics."

Because I was a detective, and because I was in Medical, the shipmind's reply was swift. *Oh dear*, said the *Fairweather*. *Is that truly necessary, Miss Gentleman?* Genetic patterns, like passengers' memories, were some of the most closely guarded data on board ship: It was rare for even a detective to have reason to open them up.

"I'm afraid so," I sighed. "We need you to find us the father of this baby."

A pause. *What baby, Miss Gentleman? Babies are not permitted while in transit.*

I opened my mouth, then closed it again. Ruthie looked as flummoxed as I felt, staring down at the baby as though he were looking at a tiny, adorable ghost.

John's lips quirked in a way that somehow mingled both amusement and exhaustion. Poor man, he really deserved a nap. "Ferry, how many people are in this room right now?"

I sense three, Mr. Pengelly.

Now we all looked at the baby. "Ferry," I said slowly, "how many hearts are beating in this room?"

Another pause, then: *Oh shit.*

I shot a glance at my nephew, who had the grace to blush. "So you taught the shipmind how to curse?" I asked.

"It seemed prudish not to," Ruthie muttered, color splashing high on his sharp cheekbones.

Ferry's agitation distracted me. *Why are there four hearts and only three people?!*

"The thing is, Ferry," I said, "someone's made a baby. Not built one—made one. Do you see?"

Every time a body was reconstituted in Medical, it was rebuilt at the age of twenty. Nobody had wanted to go through puberty multiple times, not if they could avoid it. And every single cell of every new body had a tiny little something extra built in, a little molecular scrap that Ferry could use to sense and communicate with. And, occasionally, as I had personal reason to know: to control. But only in the most exigent circumstances.

But this freshly produced child had none of that extra material. He was, to Ferry's very specialized senses, invisible. What eyes Ferry did have were focused outward, scanning for asteroids and planets and other dangers of the vastness around us. The ship could no more look casually at its insides than I could.

But the ship did have a wealth of other internal sensors,

in case of depressurization or malfunction in the artificial gravity or an impact that might threaten the integrity of the hull. It made Ferry quite sensitive to vibrations. Such as, for example, the difference between three and four hearts beating in a single room.

"We need you to tell us who made this baby," I said.

So you can stop them from making any more? Ferry demanded plaintively.

"Well—yes," I conceded. We were probably going to have to ask the parents not to produce any more children with their current bodies. We simply weren't set up to handle them.

Of course, that was presuming this baby had happened by accident, and not as a result of careful and deliberate planning. Flora, certainly, did not seem to have intended it—but Flora was not the only parent. Perhaps someone else had found a way to undo all our fertility restrictions. Perhaps everyone was going to end up pregnant and the ship's population would skyrocket. We could feed everyone with the autochefs, of course, but finding places for so many new people to live was going to be a disaster...

I reined myself in. It'd been less than a day since this mess began, but perhaps I was already spending too much time near the flickers. Stories that powerful had a way of warping perspectives. Even mine.

Please deposit part of the baby in the salvage bin, said Ferry.

Well, that was no way to maintain calm: It took five full minutes for John and me to persuade Ruthie not to flee the hospital and go on the lam to protect the child from dissection by a malicious machine. "I'm sure we could just use a lock of hair, Ruthie."

"Or . . ." John pulled up a fresh nappie from his bag and waggled it demonstratively.

I narrowed my eyes at the baby, who blinked up at me with the satisfied look of a creature that had had two full bottles of milk and plenty of time to process them.

And so the soiled nappie went into the salvage bin, and the baby's wild and feathery hair remained on his head. I popped the mess into the intake with a creak of metal and glowered through the glass as it began to glow and dissolve.

"Ferry," I said while we waited, "how many hearts are beating on the ship at present?"

Nine thousand, eight hundred, and seventy-three, the ship said after a moment. Relief was plain in his mental voice. *Not counting the seventeen in Medical that have been built but aren't active yet.*

I breathed out, and some of my fear ebbed away. John looked positively ecstatic. So our population boom really was an increase of only one. An accident rather than an influx.

A few seconds after that, Ferry revealed the child's parentage.

FLORA WAS THE mother, no surprise there.

The father, it turned out, was not the insufferable Jason Ipcar—it was Hugh Renois, an accountant who mostly worked with the projectionists and the live theaters of Aft Port Eleven and so had an office on that deck. He wore half-moon spectacles and an extremely loud floral waistcoat, and when we showed up with the baby he sat back and polished the one upon the other in the gentlest expression of shock. "Oh my word!" he said. "How curious. A child, you say? My child?"

"You didn't know?" I was watching him closely: He was not particularly expressive, but his astonishment when Ruthie had plunked the baby's basket down onto his desk had seemed genuine enough.

He returned his spectacles to their perch upon his stout nose. "Mine, and—Flora's?" he asked, then *tsk*ed at himself.

"It would have to be Flora—there hasn't been anyone else. Not in years." For a moment, those half-moons gleamed sadly as his head turned aside, but then he rallied. "Is she all right? Has something happened?"

"Why would you ask that?" I returned.

He blinked at me. "Well, I assume you wouldn't be talking to me if you could be talking to her. She's the one who would be at risk, surely?" He tugged the hem of his waistcoat and smoothed his lack of hair. "Was it—did she—was it on purpose? The pregnancy?" He swallowed. "Only I hope she'd know that if she'd wanted—if she'd asked, I'd have . . ." He trailed off with an unhappy expression.

I wondered if Flora knew how many broken hearts she was leaving in her wake. I counted two so far, which wasn't so many, except that it represented 100 percent of the people we'd talked to in Flora's life. "When was the last time you spoke to her?" I asked.

"Oh," he said with a sigh, "that would be—second quarter, last year. She and Anne—Mrs. Godfrey, I assume you've met her?—were celebrating the Palace's fifth anniversary. They held quite a party, and the memory cocktails Flora decanted were exquisite. Especially the Savoy Saturday night—made you feel like you were at the best and most luxurious party in the world just before midnight, when everyone is tipsy enough to be brave but not yet drunk enough to be obnoxious. Flora was wearing silver spangles, and I asked her to dance, and, well..." He shrugged, pinkening, and ducked his head. "I shall leave out the details, if that's all right."

"And it was only the one time?"

Mr. Renois tugged his waistcoat again, the blush deepening. "I woke up alone in her bed. Apparently she had an early matinee at some other theater that she was very keen on seeing. Flora loves the flickers more than anyone else I know... I went to the kitchen to make myself some breakfast from the autochef and Anne was there. Now, I quite like Mrs. Godfrey, but that morning she didn't seem to like me very much. I've been her bookkeeper for three out of those five years and never found her less than pleasant—but that morning, she was entirely different. Awkward, silent—not cruel, I don't think she has cruelty in her, but—well, it was very apparent that she wanted not to be resenting my presence so much. And then she looked up, and her face changed, like a light that was out had come back on. And I turned to see Flora standing behind me in the doorway. Later, I got Flora alone, thanked her for a lovely evening, and made it clear that I understood it was only a one-off. She seemed relieved, and I stayed away from the Palace except when Anne came here for business reasons." He lifted one shoulder. "You see how it is."

"What?" Ruthie demanded. "How what is? I don't see anything."

I bit back a sigh. I was going to have to find a way to abandon my sidekicks, and soon. "Mrs. Godfrey is in love with Miss Tilburn, Ruthie," I said. "Mr. Renois is explaining that he knew it, and did not pursue Miss Tilburn because of it."

"It seemed prudent to bow out gracefully, avoid the trouble before it started," Mr. Renois confirmed.

That was the kind of sensible thing that everyone knew was wise and virtually nobody ever actually did. Perhaps I should keep Mr. Renois in mind as an aberration, in case he was the solution to any of the puzzles in this case.

But there were still a few more questions to resolve: "Would you like to claim custody of the baby?" I asked. "We still have to sort things out officially, but if you are interested then we can include you in the process going forward."

He reared ever so slightly back in his chair. "Custody! Oh no, I don't think so. I'm generally a very solitary kind of person, even when people aren't babies." He gazed at the basket as one would a nest of small, nonvenomous snakes: mild wariness but not outright fear. "Would I be permitted to arrange visitation, instead of custody?"

Ruthie was ruffling like a chicken in a rainstorm, but I cut him off before he could explode. "We'll see what we can do," I replied. And now, the more delicate question: "Would you be willing to report to Medical for an examination, so we can determine how the pregnancy happened, and how to prevent future occurrences?"

"I should hardly think that necessary—Flora was, um,

an aberration from my usual habits—but if it would help, then of course."

"I'm sure the Board will appreciate it," I said, and rose to my feet.

So there we had it: one child, two parents, all properly identified and informed and promising not to do it again. The most urgent matter had been addressed. But there were still too many questions left for me to count the business as resolved—the most glaring one being, of course: Who had been the person caring for the baby after Flora had her stroke?

Who else had known about the child?

We paused outside Mr. Renois's office, bathed in the rainbow glow of Aft Port Eleven. Ruthie had the baby out of the basket and cradled on his shoulder; he swayed softly back and forth as the marquee lights tinted his face and the child's half yellow and half blue.

Perhaps that was why the sausage vendor across the deck didn't notice the baby right away—until the thing raised his head and gave a happy, hungry shriek.

The sausage vendor stared at the small blue-yellow face and shrieked back.

"Time to go," I said firmly.

We hurried into the nearest lift, and Ruthie spun to face me, still clutching the child in possessive hands. "Aunt Dorothy, I'm officially petitioning for custody."

"What?" John blurted.

I pinched the bridge of my nose and leaned against the lift wall. "Of course you are."

"Someone has to love him," my nephew said stubbornly. "If his parents aren't going to do it, then someone else has to pick up the slack. He deserves nothing less." His hand loomed large where it spread across the baby's back. He cast John a glance that was half defiance, half pleading. "I loved him the instant I saw him on our doorstep."

John's face softened. "I know you did."

"We still haven't found out who was taking care of him during the two days Flora was in Medical being reembodied," I said. "Maybe someone else already wants him."

"We could put out a bulletin," John said, but without conviction.

For a moment I winced at the prospect of telling the whole ship's population that there was a new person on board. That babies could happen, in spite of everything. It was never wise to give the passengers *ideas*. Some of them would immediately want babies of their own, and they wouldn't stop there. They were going to start questioning restrictions on everything. What would be next: Candles? Poisons?

Weapons?

Ruthie's grip on the baby tightened; the infant made a noise of protest. Ruthie murmured soothingly and bounced him a little.

I had to admit, the child did look—comfortable, there on my nephew's shoulder.

Ruthie's eyes met mine. They were the same eyes my sister had had, back on Earth. And right now they had the same set look she would get sometimes, when no amount of arguing or logic or good sense was going to change her mind.

I yielded to the inevitable. Would save me trouble in the long run, or so I hoped. "Tell you what: We'll leave the custody question aside for now. But—" I said, holding up a hand against my nephew's protests, "*for now*, I will let you pick the name we put on his paperwork."

"Peregrine," Ruthie said at once. He rested his chin briefly against the top of the infant's head. "Because he's a wanderer."

Well.

I cleared my throat, and a second time for good measure. John Pengelly sucked in a small, helpless breath, and if he raised his hand to swipe briefly at the corner of one eye I very carefully took no notice.

BACK AT THE Bureau, the day was officially in full swing, everyone present and accounted for.

Baxenden was at his desk, humming into his mustache while comparing a spectrum of lipstick samples on small cards in his stout hands. Forensics of materials was something of a specialty of his. He'd been a bricklayer once, before finding a body hidden in a wall and asking the kind of questions that annoyed the kind of people who left bodies in walls. Embarking on the *Fairweather* had saved his life and given him a new profession; he'd been the first ship's detective to sign up.

Behind the glass of his office wall, Ogilvy had a book over his gorgeous face—a true potboiler, from the look of it—but the sounds coming from under the pages were defined and definite snores. Must be between theft cases, or else he'd be retromatting some kind of mulch for the potted palm or pollinating one of the seventeen species of orchid in his office hothouse.

Next door, Mortimer Dellow, tall and authoritative with skin like umber, was carefully scraping flakes of paint from some Old Master–ish thing I didn't recognize. There were a few real antiques aboard the *Fairweather*, so every now and then someone retromatted a copy and tried to claim it as an original Earth piece. The hard part wasn't identifying the forgeries—retromatted paint was molecularly marked, after all—but getting the victim to admit they'd been deceived in the first place. Embarrassment covered up nearly as many crimes as guilt did.

Mortimer had an air of frigid capability, like a vampire or a solicitor, but underneath it was a heart that beat with even more warmth than Ruthie's, and he had an instinct for people's hidden wounds that made him one of the kindest men I knew.

Meherbai and Leloup had dug in at opposite long sides of the research table. She was flipping through a volume I recognized as the Bureau's official copy of the *Fairweather*'s legal compendium—the complete one, which covered not only the on-board regulations we were presently operating under, but the much more complex and multivalent codes that would become law only when we made planetfall. Base system of government, processes for adding laws we'd found useful on the journey, franchise rights and restrictions, the whole life-changing, mind-numbing weight of bureaucracy and justice. Insofar as we'd managed to describe it, at any rate.

Meherbai tended to see the law as clothing: Proper fit was important, so alterations could be made in service of comfort and safety. A skilled tailor could make something so elegantly fitted that the body wouldn't even feel it was constrained.

Leloup, on the other hand, tended to view the law as a scalpel, which he used to carve away the parts of people that didn't fit the law's ideal shape.

Personally, I took offense at that. Because my specialty was memory crimes, which was a fancy way of saying it was my job to make sure people kept all the most essential parts of themselves. Once upon a time, in my former life, I'd done crossword puzzles to keep my mind limber; now, I decoded people the same way, letter by letter, until the whole array became clear.

And the more I understood people, the less I liked it when someone wanted them to all be precisely the same. Leloup found comfort in predictability, in routine, and more than anything else he believed the world existed for him to be comfortable in.

I had decided centuries ago: My calling was to bedevil him at every possible opportunity.

It certainly looked like I was doing a bang-up job of

it today: He had removed his jacket and rolled up his shirtsleeves—I'd have sworn he'd even managed to press them in place somehow, so precisely identical were both folded-over cuffs—and was beetling his brows at Meherbai. "The precedents for punishing stowaways are many and date back to the Architects themselves, Miss Petit—"

"That's because we found the last stowaway three centuries ago, after a whole month on board," Meherbai retorted. "And those were deliberate crimes—I don't think you can argue this child *intended* to stow away." She twirled her enamel fountain pen with a flourish. "Unless you want to make the claim that every gamete on board the *Fairweather* is a stowaway *in potentia*."

Leloup sniffed. "I'm sure I don't wish to discuss gametes at all unless compelled to. There should be no need, when all our bodies are built. There are consequently only three possible ways to identify a new person on board: one, as a stowaway; two, as a fraud—which I think would also require intention, wouldn't you agree?—or three, as an automaton, a created thing." His eyes kindled. "Now there's a thought—there are quite a few regulations on the books for automata—"

"Am I allowed an opinion?" I interrupted. "Or is this a legal matter above my fumbling understanding?"

"You cannot understand," Leloup went on, mopping his brow, "because there is no procedure to be understood—"

"But there is," I said. "There is a very carefully crafted procedure for creating a new identity for a new person. We just didn't expect to need it for a few hundred years yet."

Meherbai lit up and began flipping to the back of the compendium.

Leloup gaped at me as if I'd suggested something utterly degenerate. Like cannibalism. Or fun. "We cannot just pull planetary law forward at our own convenience! It was intended for a very particular political situation and moment in time. It is not a chess piece to be moved about for a player's advantage."

"But it's already on the books, and I think people will find that reassuring," I countered. "The baby is going to be shocking enough to most passengers; anything we can do to make it less disruptive will surely be of use."

Leloup's mustache was trembling like a butterfly about to cause the storm of the century. "You think we should tell them about the baby."

I narrowed my eyes at him. "You think we can keep a whole human hidden from them until he turns twenty? And then just pretend he's always been here?"

Leloup fussed at his perfectly rolled cuffs and smoothed the sharp points of his shirt collar. "I think telling the passengers that someone has given birth will be a disaster for civil order and general calm."

Even though I'd had much the same thought, hearing it

come out of my nemesis's mouth turned my opinion around a full 180 degrees. "Well, we know we have to tell the Board of Directors," I began. "And possibly the Crime Committee."

"Offense: one baby," Meherbai murmured, and only grinned when I glared at her.

"So that's at least twenty people who are inevitably going to find out," I went on. "When was the last time you knew twenty people who could all keep the same secret?"

Leloup drew himself up. "Frequently, Miss Gentleman!" He raised a hand and began listing them off. "The Board's backup memory-books, the Hotchkiss Incident, the comet we had to turn to avoid— *What* is so blasted amusing, may I ask?"

For I was laughing at him helplessly, a sputtering chortle he clearly found offensive. "You just listed off a series of supposedly secret things every passenger on this ship definitely knows about—to prove that the Board is *discreet*?"

"Ugh, very well." Leloup rose to his feet with all the wounded majesty of a monarch who had just been dethroned by his own barons. "You want the passengers to be told? You may tell them. And I will direct to you all the inquiries that result—all questions about reproductive regulations, risks of the baby, risks *to* the baby, and other forbidden things people now want to try and other fail-safes they worry might also not work. Oh." He paused, and a hint of a smile slithered over his lips. "And also yours? All the paperwork."

Well. That knocked the amusement right out of me.

"And, of course..." Leloup's smile grew, oozing self-satisfaction. "If you're going to give this baby all the rights of planetary identity, then he must be given their restrictions as well. No Library access. No memory-book. No new embodiments." His eyes gleamed, glacial and smug. "When he dies, he dies."

With that finishing blow, Leloup retreated to the right-angled safety and solitude of his office.

Meherbai pushed the law book my way. "Another cup of chai?" she asked sympathetically.

"Please," I said, shivering. "I could use the warmth."

She moved toward the kitchenette, and I went looking for the first batch of forms.

HOURS LATER, WRIST cramping, I had a stack of paper solidly two inches high: an initial report to the Board about the baby, with a full write-up of his parentage; petition to the Board to use the planetside identity procedures to establish young Peregrine's legal existence; request for an exception to those procedures to allow the child to have a memory-book and right to reembodiment in Medical; written acknowledgment that I planned to ask Flora Tilburn and Hugh Renois to report to Medical for examination to find out how the pregnancy had happened and if something like it was likely to happen again; first draft of a ship-wide announcement of the baby's existence, including a reiteration of the restrictions upon childbearing and reproduction; and a custody petition form for Rutherford Talmadge IV and John Pengelly.

That last piece of paperwork alone had taken me an hour

to concoct from the few times something like it had been required in those first chaotic decades on board ship. Now that we'd all been adults for several centuries, things like custody and adoption had simply ceased to come up in the course of ordinary events. I did the best I could with the legal phrasing, shook out my aching hand, and walked through the *Fairweather*'s version of twilight down to my nephew's apartment.

NO KNOCKING, said the sign that had been hastily taped to the door. ABSOLUTELY NO KNOCKING, YES THIS MEANS YOU.

I stifled a smile, passed my thumb over the lock, and let myself in.

And froze, breath catching.

The baby was sleeping. Curled up in the crook of my nephew's arm, wrapped in a blanket. Snoring softly, with tiny motions of his fists and occasional small smackings of the mouth. Above him, slouched in the armchair, brow lightly creased and under eyes lightly smudged with fatigue, Ruthie whistled out a snore of his own. His plaid tie askew, his sweater-vest hillocked up, his shirtsleeves creased beyond the bounds of all politeness. The baby looked preternaturally angelic in slumber; my nephew looked as though he'd been bedeviled into complete and utter exhaustion.

For a moment, I simply stood there watching the little mouth make silent, sleepy chewing shapes. For all I'd been unsettled by the idea of him, a baby created farther away from Earth than any baby before . . . Well, now he was here, and he was human, and that was that. Ruthie already loved him; how could I help following suit?

Soft water sounds came from the doorway on the room's far side. I tiptoed carefully past the sleeping pair and found John in the kitchen.

My nephew-in-law was hand-washing his cashmere blanket in the sink. I waved a silent hello when he looked around. "I've brought you some forms for signatures," I murmured. "That is, if you haven't rebelled against Ruthie's demand for custody."

John looked briefly wistful, then shook his head. "When you love someone who deserves it, you have to be willing to adapt a little. I had thought I wouldn't have to think about children until planetfall, but . . ." He stopped, wistfulness turning warmer as he gazed off into the distance above the kitchen sink. "Ruthie was up most of the night with him. No bitterness, no hesitation." He swirled the fabric in the soap, suds catching the light with tiny, fragile rainbows. "I had gotten into the habit of thinking myself the practical one," he said. "But what Ruthie—and Peregrine—have taught me today is that there are kinds of practicality in which I am a fumbling amateur, and Ruthie is something of a savant."

"Ruthie has a way of upending assumptions," I said. "It's one of his virtues."

"One of his best." John rinsed the soap away and let the liquid drain out. Strong hands pressed the water from the cashmere fabric, careful not to twist the delicate fibers. He spread one corner out, turning it back and forth in the light. "I think I got most of the stains out, happy to say."

"Why not just retromat a new blanket?"

His eyes crinkled with a sly smile. "This one isn't retromatted."

"Not—you mean—" I gaped. Apparently my nephew's husband was laundering a priceless antique in his kitchen sink. He rolled the blanket up in a towel, his hands careful, almost reverent, even as they pressed more water out with sure and steady pressure.

We'd all been permitted one Earth object when we embarked—heirlooms, we called them. Some were personal mementoes, some were valuables, but all of them were something physical from the planet of our origin, something real, something more than a memory of Old Earth. Every person should have something like that. Especially someone who had no chance at those memories in the first place.

It haunted me as I walked home beneath the stretching trees.

I'd felt old even when we first embarked; after so long,

the thought of starting fresh—of being someone who hadn't made any memories yet—was more than a little horrifying. We didn't have poverty on board the *Fairweather*—that was rather the point—but the thought of less than a year's worth of memory felt like the nearest thing to it.

This must be why you brought a new baby gifts, I realized. You wrapped them in blankets because you wished you could wrap them in knowledge; you showered them with clothes and soft things because you couldn't shower them with the learned experience of your years and decades. It's why people liked handmade things for infants, even when those makes had faults.

So, exhausted though I was, I walked right past my door and a little way down the street, to the yarn store run by Violet St. Owen. A passenger's personal wealth went back into the General Fund at their death, but shared business assets remained; this worked reasonably well to encourage people to create stores and communal services rather than simply hoard cash individually. Violet's previous co-owner was now gone—an event I'd had an unfortunately close connection to—and an impulse to atone for my involvement had led me to become Violet's silent investor.

It was an easy enough job, since she asked literally nothing of me. Possibly because she was afraid of what a nosy and sharp-eyed detective would find if she went poking around.

There were people who turned to crime for profit, and

there were people who turned to crime for fun. Violet was something closer to the latter, as far as I could guess—except that instead of reveling in the killer's illicit thrills or the liar's glee in deception, she considered crime something of a righteous vocation. A democratic impulse for chaos and unruliness. A way to take power back from the authorities and share it around a little, she'd once explained, when we'd had occasion to discuss the ethics of killing in self-defense.

I had my doubts about her philosophy, personally, but she hadn't ended up being a murderess that time, and I'd never been able to concretely prove her involvement in anything else. So we waltzed round each other, suspecting but never certain, retreating when the other advanced, never making contact but never more than a breath away, either.

Maybe if I'd trusted her more, I'd have taken her to bed a year ago when we first met. Maybe if she trusted anyone at all, she'd have let me.

In addition to possible crime, she definitely ran the best yarn store on the entire *Fairweather*. Either one would have been enough to fascinate me: Together, they made her more irresistible than all her golden hair and sultry smiles. Though I was far from indifferent to those, too.

She sent me just such a smile as I entered her shop beneath the familiar ding of the bell. Her skirt was ankle-length and black; her ochre cardigan a long, luxurious drape of lace-weight yarn with a complex pattern of fans. Her hands were busy with something in a wool the exact shade of a pomegranate's heart, as though she were trying to knit with a skein of temptation itself.

"Hullo, Violet," I said. "Planned any murders lately?"

"Oh, scads," she replied. "I hope you've come to take me into custody?" And she cheekily presented her wrists for the handcuffs. The skin at the base of her palms looked velvet-soft, the tendons strong beneath from years of skill and practice. I wanted to trace them with my tongue, feel them tense and tighten.

I must have been staring, because she smiled smugly and picked up her knitting again. "How can I help a ship's detective today?"

"I'm looking for a pattern," I said, getting my tongue back under control.

"Aren't you always." She glanced at me sloe-eyed. "What kind of pattern?"

"Something small. Rectangular. Soft, so as not to irritate delicate skin."

I was teasing, dangling a secret like a locket on a chain, and Violet could tell. She narrowed her eyes and leaned on sharp elbows. "Whose delicate skin?"

"Someone new."

"I see." Her face showed no reaction, but one finger tap, tap, tapped on the glass of the countertop. "Perhaps you could describe this object more specifically?" Said the same way an interrogator might ask *And just where were you on the night of November the twenty-fourth?*

"Well, that's the difficulty. I'm not certain you carry this kind of pattern." She was glowering at me now, certain I was up to something but not able to deduce what. I couldn't help it: A grin broke out despite my best efforts to repress it. "It must be hundreds of years since anyone asked you for a baby blanket."

"For a—" She gasped. "Are you telling me someone's gone and made a baby? *Here?*"

"They absolutely have."

And Violet St. Owen threw her head back and laughed in delight.

Oh, I shouldn't have liked making her laugh so much. But I did—the pleasure of it spread warmth through my chest, sweet as honey and twice as clinging. I'd better be careful or I'd never get free.

Violet sighed in pleasure. "My dear detective, that's the opposite of a murder! However did it happen?" she asked, when at last she got hold of herself.

I leaned on the counter, smirking. "Wouldn't you like to know."

"I absolutely would," she confirmed. "People are always asking."

"People ask a yarn store proprietor about how to have babies?"

She lowered those knowing eyes beneath her lashes, looking demure and humble and a lot of other descriptors that weren't true. "I hear things, is all. You know that's one of the rules people are most excited to break, once we're planetside?"

"It won't be a rule then," I objected.

"It will still feel like one. Like they're doing something forbidden, except there won't be consequences for them to worry about. The purest kind of thrill." I could think of others, but I wasn't about to say so. Violet went on, "I predict a veritable explosion of infants that first year just as soon as people can pop them out."

"Well *that's* an image."

She cocked a head at me. "You don't want to be a parent?"

"Being an aunt suits me better," I said. Then paused. Then gathered my courage. Then went on. "You?"

"Oh." She laughed, with the kind of inward sting that one reserved for one's worst decisions. "I'm long since done with all of that."

I wasn't going to ask for the story. Not now, not here. But my not-asking was extremely loud in the silence that followed.

Violet St. Owen sailed the conversation blithely past the gap. "Are you going to have to convene the Crime Committee, do you think?"

Now it was my turn to dread a question, it seemed. I shouldn't tell her anything. "I'm not certain," I confessed instead. "It doesn't appear to have been done on purpose."

"So not retromatted? Or cloned?" Her eyes widened. "You mean someone carried it for nine months? In space?" She paled, and her voice trembled. "Is she . . . ?"

"She's just gotten out of Medical," I said. "Reembodied. Though the baby was born five months ago."

She chewed her lip. "So it wasn't the birth that did it?"

"She said she had some kind of stroke."

"That happened to my sister, when she gave birth to my niece." It was barely more than a whisper.

Her too-careful expression was like a knife to my heart; I had to blunt that edge. "Ruthie's petitioning for custody," I said.

I'd hoped to make her laugh again, but instead she simply relaxed, resting her forearms on the counter and slumping over them as if some thread running through her had been snipped free. "Glad to hear someone in all this is being sensible. Ruthie's exactly who I'd want to have raising a child."

"Really?" I asked. "My nephew? Tallish, brown hair, once forgot to eat or bathe for two days because he was excited about a script he'd written for the shipmind? That Ruthie?"

"Of course. It's something of a running joke, you know, at the Antikythera Club."

"I didn't realize you were a member."

Her smirk overflowed with secrets as she leaned forward. "I'm not."

"You just hear things," I breathed.

She nodded. "Everyone knows your nephew is the best scriptwriter on this ship. And the Antikythera Club knows why: because he's good at breaking a complicated process down into simpler steps. The *Fairweather* is an extraordinary creature, really. Adaptable. Which is to say: The shipmind can learn, and grow. It's not so much that your nephew gives Ferry commands—it's more like he's teaching the shipmind how to solve its own problems." That tempting mouth of hers turned up at the corners. "So from a certain point of view, Ruthie's been a parent for three centuries now. How much more practice could someone need?"

"I'm fairly sure the nappies were a novel experience." Violet laughed again, and something strained in me relaxed its fibers and unknotted. "We're calling the baby Peregrine, until he tells us otherwise."

"Then let's find you some yarn for the tyke."

I came away with a stitch chart I could adapt to fit our new small human, as well as several skeins of a cotton so soft it practically floated, in shades of blue from sky to midnight, and one of silver so I could pick out stars in duplicate stitch. After a good dinner and with a glass of port to hand, I cozied up in my bedroom window seat on the upper story, casting on the first row while the neighborhood all around me enjoyed its evening.

One stitch for the young woman playing violin on the corner, the echoes singing up and down the decks. One stitch each for the two young men strolling arm in arm out of a restaurant. Trios and groups, friends and families, I counted them all out beneath my hands as the solar lamps dimmed and the storefronts spilled gold light onto the retromatted wood planks.

One stitch each, every stitch a second, a single moment in time frozen in fiber. To give to an infant—because time was the real gift, passed from one generation to the next.

It was easy to think that time was infinite, here on the *Fairweather*. Your body wore out and was replaced; your memories were refreshed with a sip of a drink or the press of a button. Easy to think we were standing still—but really, we were flying through the universe at incredible speeds. And the same end was waiting for us that would have met us on Old Earth. It was just going to take a little longer to get there, that was all.

The faint sound of a bell, and a pair of furtive silhouettes slipped into Violet's store. Fellow honest knitters like myself? Or passengers more like Violet, with dangerous ideas about power and the law?

I thought the law was the necessary foundation of a solid society; she thought the authorities weren't to be trusted with too much power. If she was right, then I was wrong, and that rankled. But if I was right, and Violet was wrong—then why did I still want her so much?

I knit until I was sure the question wouldn't keep me awake.

DOROTHY!

The shipmind's mental voice erupted into my dreams and dragged me into unwilling wakefulness. "Whuzzat? Ferry?" I said, trying to grasp the reins of thoughts that had been galloping elsewhere a moment before.

Your nephew is on the way over, Ferry went on, words tumbling over themselves like a shower of pebbles in my mind. *He said to wake you immediately.* The shipmind coughed, a trick it had picked up from Ruthie himself when there was something unpleasant to say. *I think there's a problem with the child.*

"You think?" I asked, before logic caught up with me. "No, of course, you wouldn't be able to tell, would you?"

I think I might, in time, Ferry went on. *A few years, perhaps? When he's eaten and drunk enough retromatted food that his body holds on to the molecular markers.*

Well that was an image to haunt one, for certain. I imagined Peregrine's toddler shape amorphous and misty, like the ghost of a child wandering the darkened decks.

I shivered involuntarily.

It was just before dawn, according to the nocturnal blue glow of the solar lamps. They dyed my fern shawl shadow colors as I flung it over my pyjamas and took my place in the window seat. Soon enough a pair of huddled figures appeared on the corner, breezing behind a drunk woman lounging on a bench overlooking the Greenway. Peregrine's wails were audible even with my doors and windows shut, and I saw the woman's head swivel around and her whole body tilt sideways, trying to follow the unwonted sound of a crying child in a place no child should be.

I hurried downstairs and wrenched open the front door.

Ruthie and John and Peregrine barged in, Ruthie wild-eyed and clutching the howling infant to his shoulder. John immediately locked the door behind them, checked the curtains were snug, and went to the kitchen to perform the same ritual there.

"Honestly," I said, rubbing the grit from my eyes and hoping the rest of the neighborhood had either slept through the racket or failed to identify the source. "We're going to have to teach you fellows what lullabies are for."

Ruthie didn't so much as crack a smile. "Someone tried to take Peregrine."

That woke me up, and no mistake. "What? When? Who?"

"Half an hour ago. No idea who."

John came back out of the kitchen and guided Ruthie into a chair. Ruthie sat without looking down, his face drawn and his knuckles white.

Baby Peregrine yowled and beat at one shoulder with his tiny fists. I could feel a slight hum at the very edges of my mind, which meant Ferry was probably still listening in.

"Here," John said, and reached for the child.

Ruthie made a noise like he would reject this, then visibly forced himself to let go and gave the baby to his husband. John began pacing the living room, making soothing sounds.

I sat in the other armchair and picked up my knitting; it would give my hands something to fidget with until the crying stopped.

We were lucky: Not five minutes later, the baby was snoring and drooling into John's coat seams. Wisely, he kept bouncing.

Ruthie leaned forward, pitching his voice low. "After we left Medical, I sat down to rest my eyes a moment in the living room, while John washed his blanket. He tells me you stopped by with paperwork sometime after that?"

"That's right."

"Well, I slept through you, and I just kept on sleeping.

All the advice I've been reading says that when the baby sleeps, you should sleep, too. So I did. John stayed up a bit reading over dinner, then headed upstairs for a shower. He checked on us again, and then decided to get some sleep himself." Ruthie swallowed. "And then, next thing I know, I'm waking up and the door is open and there's someone standing over me, reaching for Peregrine."

I shuddered. "Description?"

"Thought it was a man. Short hair, men's jacket, thin build. His face was in shadow from the light coming in the door behind him. And then . . ." He wheezed out the ghost of a laugh. "Peregrine woke up. And he did not want to. And he began to protest."

"I heard him from upstairs," John put in as he continued to circuit the room.

"And the kidnapper didn't expect it, because he jerked back." Ruthie's face turned smug beneath the pallor. "And then *I* began to protest. Rather strenuously. With a fist."

"You hit him?"

"Unfortunately, no—it is quite hard to issue a decisive and shattering blow to an enemy's jawbone when you are trying to do it around a very loud, very fragile baby. But I was going in for a second attempt anyway, and this one would have been a face ruiner."

"And a hand ruiner," John muttered.

"The intruder turned and ran—John chased him a ways

down the deck, but lost him when he turned into the Greenway."

"The lock was wiped when he entered," John added. "So we can't trace him that way."

And I couldn't help, either, Ferry added plaintively. The shipmind could be queried about any individual's present location, but for privacy's sake didn't store records of passenger movement. And there were a hundred perfectly legitimate, innocent reasons why a person would be in the Greenway in the middle of the night.

"So we decided to come here," Ruthie finished. "Because what good is having an aunt for a ship's detective if you have to do all your own detecting?" He planted his hands on his knees and sat up in the armchair. "I demand a full investigation into Crimes Committed and their potential involvement in the first attempted kidnapping of a minor that the *Fairweather* has seen in three hundred years."

Oh, stars save us.

I dropped my head into my hands. Crimes Committed was a myth from the Antikythera Club, a running joke about some mysterious villain who collected all the dangerous inventions and frightening schemes club members created (when they weren't dreaming up useful technology and advancing scientific knowledge, which devices were naturally passed along to the Board). If Crimes Committed was real, that was probably what Violet was up to—but I didn't want to think Violet would ever be a menace to my family. "Allow me to investigate on my own, please, Ruthie. The three of you can stay here—I'll ask for a guard, and have Ferry revoke all accesses but mine and yours until we can figure out what's happened."

Ruthie grumbled. John said, "I'll have to call in for my shift."

"Wait—don't do that," I said, as an idea occurred. John was the most talented mixer of memory cocktails at the Antikythera Club. A place of overstuffed furniture, decadent food, and wild and wide-ranging intellects. "You and Ruthie should both go in. And you should take Peregrine with you."

"I don't see how cocktails are going to help this situation," Ruthie protested, though his eyes spoke of yearning.

"Couldn't hurt," John murmured, mid-bounce.

"Think of it this way," I said. "You could stay here, alone, in a place they know you'll run to, exhausted and fearful. We already know the intruder can bypass the door locks. Or... you could take Peregrine to the Antikythera, where he will be the absolute center of at least a dozen wide-awake, brilliant people's rapt attention—and where entry is also heavily restricted and the entrance monitored around the clock."

Ruthie gave a little laugh, desperation ringing in every note of it. "Well," he said, "that settles it. Cocktails it is."

I finished my coffee, decided the ship-wide announcement couldn't wait, sent it off urgently for the Board's approval, and escorted my little trio to the Antikythera Club's doorway.

Gaskill was the door-warden on duty this morning, a broad-shouldered, stone-faced woman I'd never once seen crack a smile. She stared for a long moment at the baby, whom Ruthie had reclaimed and was holding close to his chest like a bear cradling a wayward cub.

Slowly, Gaskill leaned down and peered into the child's eyes.

Peregrine blinked up at her innocently—and burped.

Gaskill reared back with widened eyes, but thumbed open the wide front door. "Two guests," she said, her voice a low rumble. Was that an amused tilt at the corners of her mouth? "You can sign for both of you, Miss Gentleman."

"I'm not staying," I said, and so I put down Peregrine's name on the guest ledger, bid farewell to my nephew and his beloved, and walked through the brightening day to Flora Tilburn's secret apartment.

It was clearly time for a more thorough investigation of the premises.

The lock was still wiped, the food still wilted, the frocks still somehow sad on their lonely hangers. Something about sequin fabric in shadow never failed to seem tragic. I shut the closet doors and went through the bedroom—and there, between the mattress and its retromatted frame,

I found a slim hardback bound in blue cloth, almost filled with handwriting in blue ink.

Flora Tilburn had been keeping a diary.

I didn't even have to pretend I wasn't going to read it. This was an official investigation, a child's safety was at stake, and nobody was around to chide me about privacy and discretion. For once, I didn't have to feel guilty about indulging my curiosity.

So how perverse of me to feel that pang of guilt, regardless.

Flora had gone to such lengths to hide her secrets from everyone, and some part of me hated having to undo all that work and hurt her in a way she didn't deserve.

But more of me wanted to learn what she'd been up to—so into the diary I went.

Dear Diary, she began, because of course she did.

This is how they always start in the flickers, so this is how I'll begin. I need to remember everything, and now that I'm not updating my memory-book in the Library this is the only way.

Florian was born at six in the evening—the afternoon matinee would have ended, but the evening showtime wouldn't have yet begun. The best thing I can say about it is it was quicker than I'd feared. If it were only about the labor I might have slipped out from the Palace, borne down a time or two, cleaned myself up, and been back in my seat before the next showing's title cards went up—but it wasn't just that, of course.

I couldn't do that to Anne.

She's told me so much about her life before Embarkation—about losing Norris's father, and how she threw herself into being a mother for so long she forgot how to be anything else. She got started as a projectionist because she wanted to give her son a way to experience his father as more than just a name and a story, since Norris was only a boy when he died and the two of them came aboard the <u>Fairweather</u>. They bonded over their first home skimmer— Anne projecting her memories of her lost love, Norris taking the skimmer apart to learn how the tech worked—but I still think he was a little put out when we started the Palace and Anne's gifts became public knowledge. I think he liked having a secret between just the two of them.

But Anne has bloomed so much since I met her. She's happier now that she's more than a mother, I know she is. She deserves some time to be herself for a little while. And I know she'd happily help me care for Florian, and keep him safe and secret if I asked her to—but that would be like asking her to forget who she's become. How could I do that to someone I love?

Norris agrees with me for once, so I know it's the right thing to do. A mother is irreplaceable, he says, especially for a child with no father, either.

So I suppose I get to keep a secret of my own. At least for a few years, until he's grown and can make his own choices.

If I can manage it, that is. My new son is loud. *Norris assures me that the soundproofing is very good, that none of the neighbors are going to hear Florian no matter how shouty he gets. I don't know what I'm going to do when he's old enough to learn to work the doors. I've had nightmares about him escaping to wander the ship, among all those people out there who are bigger and older and stronger than him. With no memory-book waiting for him if something should go wrong.*

I have to keep him entertained to keep him safe.

Norris is not who I'd have picked to help me, but he's the one who figured out why I'd been feeling so ill, so there was no hiding it from him. He's been awfully sweet about it, even bringing me a skimmer so I can project things for Florian. I haven't Anne's talents, it's clear: I have to work to keep the figures consistent, to keep the pictures steady and the stories from rushing ahead too quickly. How does she manage it without going mad? Last month it was Busby Berkeley, three times a day! I feel queasy just thinking about it.

Norris suggested I stick to my own memories rather than movies—apparently the stronger the emotion, the clearer the projection—so I'm projecting paintings I remember, illustrations brought to life, children's stories my mother used to read to me on Old Earth. Things I can sing along to, make up lyrics for. He coos at "Cinderella" for the pumpkin and the party, he cries at "Sleeping Beauty" for the dragon and the thorns—my son, through and through. It's not what I'd have chosen, but it's a duty I cannot put aside.

I've been trying to project memories of Anne. The summer they let fireflies loose in the Greenway, and we spent a whole night walking through a sea of living stars. But every time I try to focus on her face, it melts and morphs into someone I don't recognize.

Or maybe it's the tears doing that, because I can hardly think of Anne without weeping. I miss her terribly. I hope that one day I can make her understand. We have centuries, after all—this is just a brief interruption. The third-act twist, where I realize how foolish I've been and how different I wish things were.

I put down the book and stepped back out to the living room. And there it was, now that I knew to look for it: a broad wall free of paintings or knickknacks, and when I stepped close so the light caught it at an angle, I could see the faint square shape where the paint had faded away beneath the repeated touch of the projector beam. The wall opposite was covered with framed photographs and landscapes—and one single glass lens, mounted discreetly among the artworks like a demure debutante's eye.

Another search failed to turn up anything like a skimmer,

however. Someone must have taken it away. The fabled Norris, perhaps?

I returned to the diary.

> *I've been rereading my earlier entries*, Flora wrote. *That bit about the fireflies?*
> *I don't remember that.*

Gooseflesh broke out on my arms and ran down the back of my neck.

> *I remember remembering it, remember exactly where I was and how I was sitting when I wrote those words—it was only two days ago—but the actual memory, that sea of stars? A blank. Nothing there at all.*
>
> *Maybe it's just the sleep deprivation. Florian has decided to cry almost constantly, and I'm fighting to stay awake and alert.*
>
> *Maybe something is wrong with me. Maybe I'm going crazy. I keep thinking I see film characters in the corners of my eyes, but then when I turn of course there's nobody there. And I haven't been to the flickers in almost six months now . . .*

I'd known new motherhood could be lonely, but this rang all my alarm bells. I made a note of the entry and forged on.

Today I went to see Jason. Florian's father.

Well, now we were getting somewhere. Jason wasn't the father, of course—but I only knew that because of Ferry. Flora would have had to make the best guess she could.

I couldn't tell him about his son directly, of course—not before I knew what he'd want. So I told him about a script I was working on, a made-up one, where someone had a baby and the parents stopped updating their memory-books so the ship wouldn't become aware of the baby's existence. It was a great sacrifice they made, I said, very beautiful. Don't you think that's beautiful?

Horrible man that he is, he <u>laughed</u>.

"I know children are supposed to be a person's legacy—but come on, Flora, memory-books are where the real immortality's at. Listen, here's how I'd write it . . ." And he made it one of his usual pieces, where the baby was a teenager forced to grow up too fast and the mother was addicted to memory cocktails and the father had to retromat a gun for some made-up reason. Jason's never even held a gun before—he was a grocery store manager on Earth before Embarkation—so I don't know why he's so romantic about them. Granted, his scenarios are quite popular with a certain set—they can even be stylish, when someone with Anne's talents is projecting them—but this only confirmed

my notion that as fun as it's been, the affair has burned itself out.

He'll have forgotten all about this conversation by next week. I'll break it off then.

I set the diary aside. Flora had thought Jason was the father, and had all but told him so. Had he seen through her hypotheticals to the truth beneath? Had he discovered the baby and felt possessive, or jealous?

It was clear I'd have to have a chat with the man. After I spoke with Flora, of course.

I left everything in the apartment as it was—but I took the diary with me. It pulled down my jacket pocket, a weight made of secrets.

BACK AT THE Palace, the poster on the window was advertising a new flicker, starting in fifteen minutes: *Alias Lady Danger*, it read, all silhouettes and shadows. A skyscraper was somehow also a burning cigarette; another was the barrel of a gun; behind them all loomed a svelte woman in a silver frock, her red lips the only spot of color in the image.

Perhaps I deserved a little respite. I nodded to Flora and Anne, and settled in for the show.

Flora's diary had been right: Anne really was a brilliant projectionist. The scenario itself was a bauble—but the faces, the costumes, the dialogue she put in brought it to life, as Flora's fingers poured out a stream of glittering notes on the piano to keep the whole thing bobbing along.

In the flicker, a lady detective had to solve the murder of a wealthy industrialist and was torn between the industrialist's dashing young heir and a quiet housemaid with a murky past.

Standard stuff, but sharply and snappily done—at the end of the film the heir had been revealed as the killer, the housemaid had been revealed as the true heiress, and she and the detective waltzed off into the sunset together.

If only real life could be so easily and quickly resolved.

The night scenes did indeed try to flip to day—little stutters in the frames, like something fighting to get free. I squinted my eyes against them defensively. Anne cleverly turned one into a thunderstorm, which turned an otherwise cliché balcony love scene into something sinister and fraught. When the lights came up I leaned back in my chair and waited.

Flora went for the hoover. A tallish older man with hair like wings over his ears moved to the back, plucking the skimmer from Anne's head. "I know just what the problem is," he said eagerly, and pulled out a slim screwdriver.

Jason Ipcar could wait: I wanted to watch this technician at work.

The inside of a skimmer was all metal pins and memory-glass tubing. I could hardly tell where anything started or finished, but Winged Hair tightened something on one side, long fingers sure and steady. "You're just too mighty for this poor device, Mother," said the man I now guessed was Norris. "Your night scenes are so vivid that you set one of the connections loose."

"Would imagining more contrast in the scene help any, if it happens again?" Anne asked. "I could always go a bit more *Caligari* with things. Or you could always teach me how to fix it myself."

"And give up my secrets? Never," Norris replied. Flora rolled her eyes and Anne laughed fondly; this had the cadence of an old and much-cherished argument. "Here," the man said, resting the skimmer on Anne's head again. "Give her a try."

The projectionist glanced around; aside from myself, the rest of the audience had wandered back out onto the deck in search of food. She caught my eye and something defiant rose up in her face. "Would you like to see the night I found the baby, Miss Gentleman?"

"Why, yes," I said, smiling serenely and ignoring the way Norris's eyes widened and Flora's shoulders stiffened at the mention of the baby. "What a good idea."

The lights went down at a touch of the projectionist's hand. And there on the wall was the *Fairweather* at night, its long decks quiescent, its solar lamps turned silver with imitation moonlight.

Flora's secret apartment loomed onscreen like a Gothic manor, as a ghostly hand I presumed was Anne Godfrey's reached out and keyed open the door with a touch. "You had access?" I asked.

"I took a chance that Flora would have programmed me into the lock," Anne said.

"Of course I would," Flora murmured.

There was the living room, a dark mass. Norris truly had repaired the skimmer, for the black was steady and unrelenting until Anne-on-screen toggled on the lights. "Gosh, that's bleak," Flora said. "Look how lonely I was without you, Anne."

"This is about when I heard the baby crying," Anne said, voice thick, and the perspective began to move quite rapidly toward the stairs to the upper story.

"Wait," I said, and pointed to a corner of the screen. "Can you show me that more clearly?"

The image paused and spooled back. Shapes on the edge were fuzzier than the center but there on a stand, beneath the lens in the wall, was a telltale brim and circle shape. Imperfectly remembered, but unmistakable.

"Does that look like a skimmer to you, Mr. Norris?" I asked.

He gazed back at me, eyes wide. "It certainly does, Miss Gentleman."

"And what if I asked you where it had gone?"

He smiled politely. "I'm sure I couldn't say."

"That *is* a skimmer." Anne's eyes sharpened as she turned to fix Flora with an accusing glance. There was only one place Flora would have gotten that equipment, and Anne and everyone else in the room knew it. "You told Norris about the baby, but you couldn't tell me."

"I didn't know how—" Flora stammered, but Anne was already turning away and striding out of the room into the kitchen. "Wait!" Flora hurried after, explanations and apologies already tumbling like rose petals from her lips.

I turned back to Norris. "You are the expert, aren't you, sir? How easy is it for one of these experiences to be falsified?" I waved my hand at the skimmer, the lens, and Anne's projected memory all together.

Norris's eye kindled, as I knew it would. What technician doesn't love to wax authoritative on their most passionate subject? "About as easy as it is to lie, more or less," he said. "They drift, the same as all human memories do, whether you're watching a projection or interrogating someone's testimony of events. And of course strongly creative, imaginative people can fill in all sorts of details that may or may not have been actually present at the time."

I nodded. "Imaginative people like your mother, you mean."

"Precisely."

"She is obviously very talented—how many people are in her league? I'm afraid I don't get around to a show as often as I'd like."

"Well," said Norris, "I confess to being biased, but in my

opinion she's the most brilliant projectionist we have on the *Fairweather*, bar none."

"Quite a compliment from someone of your caliber," I said, doing my best to sound impressed in spite of myself. A little bit of awe, a little bit of grudging reluctance. Then I slid in the rapier's point. "If she's good enough to create out of whole cloth, do you think it's possible she could uncreate as well? Use a flicker to overwrite a real memory with a false one, for instance—or even erase a memory altogether?"

Norris drew back. "How little you must think of people, Miss Gentleman. Memories are remarkably persistent. If someone sat you down and told you an obvious lie, you wouldn't throw the truth away like some flimsy piece of trash."

You might be surprised, I thought. But I said: "What if someone told you the same lie every morning, across the cozy, familiar breakfast table? Wouldn't you eventually give it some weight?"

His mouth went flat, his distaste plain. "Only if you had some reason to believe the lie. Some weakness of character, or something to gain."

And, I guessed, it would work best on subjects who were already isolated. No other interactions to undermine your programming, no counternarratives to the one you were trying to instill.

Norris was still watching me too closely. "You say you don't see many flickers, miss—so what brought you here to the Palace this afternoon?"

"Didn't your mother tell you?" I said sweetly. "I'm a ship's detective."

Norris was very good at hiding his thoughts: If I hadn't been watching for it, I'd not have seen that giveaway little flinch at all. "Can I assume you're here about the child?"

"Why else?" I replied. "How did you first learn about him?"

He cast a quick glance over his shoulder to the kitchen, whence the sounds of an argument conducted in near-whispers still reached us. "Flora'd been feeling ill and gaining weight. I'd come by to replace one of the projector lenses while my mother was out, and she passed out right in front of me. I was helping her up when the baby kicked for the first time—and we realized the truth at nearly the same moment." He shook his head. "I'll never forget the look on her face: She was clearly horrified. I'm sure I looked much the same."

"But she didn't tell her roommate?" I pressed. "Her best friend?"

"She refused to," he said. "And quite frankly, I agreed with her." He chewed his lip a bit, then leaned in. "Can I confess something to you, Miss Gentleman?"

I matched his tone. "Anything, Mr. Godfrey."

"When my mother first met Flora, I didn't react well to their friendship. She's such a flighty thing—bought a place on the *Fairweather* on a whim in her late teens, has never had a settled partner, lives for the flickers and the parties and the nightlife. The kind of butterfly lifestyle that people normally grow out of, except here she's had no reason to. And my mother was a widow who raised me all on her own. She had to scrape together every last cent to pay for our berths on this ship—but she did it, worked herself nearly to the bone just so she and I would have a better life together far away from Earth." His tone was absolutely, utterly sincere as he said: "I love her dearly, and there is nothing I would not do to keep her safe."

"And you didn't trust Flora to love her quite so well," I murmured back.

"Not at first," he confirmed, running a hand through his graying hair. "But it was clear even to me that Flora was trying. That she was doing the best she could, as the person she was. But when we realized Flora was going to become a mother—when she was looking at that level of sacrifice, of putting someone else first, of caring for a child and letting that duty transform her, shape her, transmute her into the kind of person who could do all those necessary things, out of love . . ." He shrugged. "Well, to be perfectly honest, I thought it would be good for her. She could better understand what my mother went through, could understand a child's need for stability, for constancy. It would be the thing to bring them permanently together . . . eventually."

"But you still didn't want her to tell Anne?"

He shook his head. "I know my mother well, Miss Gentleman. She'd have done everything for Flora's child. It would have come naturally to her. She'd have ended up with a second son to raise—and Flora would have gone waltzing off to the next party, blissful and unaltered."

"Truly, a terrible fate," I murmured before I could help myself. His eyes narrowed. "Thank you so much for your time, Mr. Godfrey," I went on. "I'll be sure to find you if I have any more questions about the skimmers."

"Any time, Miss Gentleman," he said, and flicked a glance at the kitchen with a sigh. "I'm afraid I have several other visits to make this afternoon—please make my farewells to my mother and to Flora?"

I promised to do so, and he gathered his things and slipped out the door.

Norris had been leading my list of suspects for the intruder who'd tried to take Peregrine—he'd known about the child, had the technical skill to breach the lock, and had the short hair Ruthie had described—but for the life of me I couldn't see any reason for him to attempt the kidnapping. Even if he'd quietly—or not so quietly—wished to separate his mother and Flora, that depended on Peregrine being kept hidden from Anne, and that level of secrecy was no longer possible.

I didn't trust him—but nor did I think he was desperate. I'd have to look further afield for my kidnapper, it seemed.

I STEPPED INTO Flora and Anne's kitchen and found myself witnessing a second very passionate kiss, in real life rather than on a screen.

Either Flora had leaned down to meet Anne, or Anne had hauled herself up to Flora's level. Either way Anne's hands were clenching the collar of Flora's shirt, and Flora's arms were tight around Anne's waist, holding her up while her mouth made a very persuasive if wordless declaration.

Good for the girls, I thought, and coughed slightly.

They broke apart, and Anne brushed hastily at her mouth and looked up at Flora with hope like a tender spring shoot in her eyes.

Flora, shaken, biffed it. "I'm so sorry," she blurted. "I didn't mean for that to happen."

I winced, unnoticed by either of them. On the list of

things nobody wants to hear after a kiss, that was pretty much at the top.

Anne's face passed from spring to winter with not a jot of summer on the way. "Excuse me, Miss Gentleman," she said, turning away from Flora. "Our next show starts in twenty minutes, and somebody needs to take tickets." And she strode out of the room with as much dignity as the situation would permit.

I turned to Flora, who was looking bewildered about the eyes and more than a little bruised about the lips. "You know, there's such a thing as being *too* careful with someone's feelings."

Flora grimaced. "That's not a problem I'm used to having."

I expect not, I thought.

"But my usual habits won't do for Anne at all," Flora went on. "She's only just moved out after three centuries of living with her son. She's only just started to figure out how brilliant she is. How could I ask her to belong to me, when she's only just learned to belong to herself?"

It was the same concern I'd read in Flora's diary. I almost pulled it out of my pocket and showed it to her—but something held me back. Not everyone took well to being confronted with a secret second self, and I wanted a little more time to tease out the diary's revelations before I let it out of my hands.

But there was one other question within my purview: "Would you like to know who the father is?"

"Not Jason Ipcar?" Flora said, her mouth going flat. "Because I broke it off with him. By note."

"Not him," I assured her.

She took a breath and nodded bravely.

"Hugh Renois."

Surprise, and relief, and something softer. "I'm glad," she said. "He's very kind, is Hugh."

"Please excuse my asking this, but . . ." I lowered my voice, though the thick curtains in the doorway would prevent anyone from overhearing unless they were very close. "Would you be willing to make an appointment with Medical for an examination? To understand how you were able to conceive in the first place, and to make certain this doesn't happen again. It would make things easier all around—until your next embodiment, of course."

"Yes," Flora said, with a pained kind of intensity. "Yes, I agree it would. It's not that I don't want to become a parent, you see—eventually. And it's one thing to discover a pregnancy. It's quite another to be handed a living child and told you're responsible. I just—I just don't feel it the same way at present, is all." She ducked her head, shame splashing red on her cheeks. "You understand?"

"Of course," I replied. People liked to think they made

choices based on reasons, but one thing I'd learned was that they made choices first, and came up with reasons after the fact. Flora had had to make this choice twice, and chose differently each time. It wasn't a fault, merely a complication. "Please let me know if any more trouble comes up."

"I will," she said, and then impulsively leaned forward and seized my hand. "You've been very good to us through all this mess, Miss Gentleman, and we appreciate it, Anne and I."

The weight of that soft hand, the intimacy of her smile—yes, Flora Tilburn was one of nature's born heartbreakers.

Good thing my heart wasn't hers to be broken. I patted her wrist genially and made my escape.

My membership application was still pending, but Gaskill allowed me entrance to the Antikythera Club with a silent nod. Alas, Ruthie and John had not taken the baby into the bar—I could have done with something stiff and sparkling—but into the cozy, cushioned warmth of the club library. Velvet chairs waited with welcoming arms to receive readers, sturdy tables stood ready to support spread-out research materials, and small burnished lamps cast warm light over hardbacks and paperbacks alike. Retromatting texts was nearly as difficult as retromatting clothing—but retromatting paper and platens and type from a set of instructions was entirely feasible, and several publishing companies currently flourished on the ship, as well as a dozen different newspapers and magazines.

I'd have guessed about half the books on these shelves had never been seen on Old Earth. Probably for the best, as the ideas Antikythera Club members tended to produce were the kind that were as beautiful and brilliant as lightning, and just as dangerous to try to grasp with a human hand.

Unless, it seemed, that hand was small and plump and belonged to the infant Peregrine, because the baby was currently at the center of an admiring circle of geniuses and being pampered like a very small, very smug Louis XIV.

A particle physicist held out one digit to be grasped by tiny baby fingers, and the *Fairweather*'s greatest astronomer was currently waggling her glasses up and down to make Peregrine giggle at the way they caught the light. Several people were whispering questions to Ruthie, and I misliked the way they were taking such careful notes. As if the baby were an object of study, a stunning scientific theory, or a newly engineered weapon, rather than a small fragile person unable to defend himself.

I found a seat near where John sat sprawled in an armchair, his hands wrapped around something with wreaths of steam. "Any news?" he asked.

"Some," I conceded. "And I have an ethical dilemma to put to you."

"It would be nice to use my brain for something other than internal screaming," John said with a glance at the baby and his court of scientists. Ruthie had produced a bottle and they were all avidly watching the baby eat, nestled in the crook of my nephew's arm, Ruthie proud and fond as any new parent.

"It seems," I said, "that Flora had stopped updating her memory-book, so as to keep Peregrine's existence a secret from Ferry."

"That girl watches too many flickers," John muttered.

I pulled the diary from my pocket and set it on the short table between us. "But she did not entirely give up recording her memories. She only switched mediums. And there's a lot in here that I don't think she'd want other people to see."

"Not a problem for a detective," John said wryly.

"Thankfully not," I answered cheerfully. "But here's my dilemma: When all the detecting is done, and the various threads of this case have been unbraided, should I give Flora her diary back? I mean, would it be a gift or a burden?"

John considered. "Is it not hers by right?"

"In one sense. In another sense it belongs to a woman who's gone. Someone who once existed, and now does not." I tucked one leg under me and leaned forward. "You heard her say she felt like it had happened to someone else. It sounded a little traumatic. I'm not at all interested in traumatizing her further."

John tapped his fingers on the blue cloth cover. "I suppose it depends on where you draw the boundary. Do we all become different people when we get reembodied in Medical?"

"Sometimes," I said.

John's eyes turned more knowing than was comfortable. "This is about Celia, isn't it?"

I always went a little breathless at the name, even all these years later. My former wife had been losing her ability to retain memories in her body—which wasn't a problem, so long as they were preserved in her memory-book in the Library. But an accident had wiped those clean, and our marriage had not survived their erasure. "I tried to tell her stories," I admitted. "To give her my own memories in place of hers. It . . . proved uncomfortable for both of us."

John nodded. "You didn't want to feel like you had that much control over her."

"I—yes," I said. It was disconcerting to have someone else be so precise and on point about something so intimate. I squirmed, feeling a new sympathy for the people I prodded with questions day in and day out. "Perhaps I'm not as meddlesome as I've come to believe."

"Let's not be hasty." I made a face at him, and John snickered into his coffee. But the speculation hadn't left those observant eyes. "Something about Flora reminds you of Celia," he said.

"I thought it was just the blond hair at first. Now I'm not so sure." Some of those diary passages kept whispering through my mind... "Perhaps I'll ask her what she would prefer," I said. "Give the decision to the person whom it most concerns, wash my hands of the whole problem."

"Probably best," John said, and finished his coffee. "And now I should probably take my turn with the baby and give my beloved time to eat something."

He rose smoothly from his chair and moved toward the little group centered on Peregrine. Efficient practice and unnaysayable authority soon had Ruthie up, a drowsy Peregrine on John's shoulder, several scientists shushed, and a soothing sense of calm returning to the space. Most of the club members wandered off, flipping through notebook pages and talking animatedly about the day's revelations.

Ruthie came over looking equal parts joyful and wrung out, like a party frock freshly washed and spread out to dry. "Hullo, Aunt," he said. "Fancy a sandwich?"

I gratefully accepted, and we decamped to the bar area, food not being permitted in the library.

The Antikythera's chef had a way with a Monte Cristo that was something close to witchcraft. I wolfed down the first half and savored the second.

Ruthie ate absently, gaze flicking over to Peregrine approximately every three seconds. "May I ask you something, Aunt Dorothy?"

I waved to indicate yes, swallowing my bite of sandwich.

"How much do you remember of my mother?"

I paused, looking at him narrowly. He was serious—as serious as my nephew ever got, anyway—and there was a light in his eyes that I hadn't seen before.

This wasn't an idle question, I realized. This was about... before. John must have told him the secret.

To be honest, I was less than surprised. John's training, like mine, meant he was aware of certain facts about the origin of our journey that were not publicly known among the *Fairweather*'s passenger population. Nothing dangerous, merely... unsettling. I'd been expecting John to fill Ruthie in at some point—honestly, when I'd learned it, I'd asked why Ruthie and the other scriptwriters hadn't been told, but had been fobbed off with some murmurings about security and discretion and other nonsense.

But now Ruthie knew, and knew that I knew. Poor John—I hoped the conversation hadn't been too hard on him.

My nephew was still waiting for my answer. I pulled together the tattered threads of ancient memories, such as remained. "You look like her," I said. "You even talk like her. I remember being at her wedding to your father, and holding her hand during the divorce trial. They were still quite scandalous proceedings then, so she moved with you to the States to raise you in a society that wouldn't hold it against you quite so much. And I remember... we had a cottage, growing up, a small thing in the farthest corner of the estate.

Meant for a hunting lodge, but Mother had it done over so it was more like a tea cake, all pastels and soft cushions. We basically lived there in summers, your mother and I."

He nodded, his eyes distant.

I braced myself and gentled my voice. "You?"

It was a while before he answered. "Her perfume," he said. "Lilacs."

I'd forgotten that, and had to catch my breath.

"I found a bottle in a shop once that smelled right. I keep it on the nightstand, so every now and then I can smell it and try to remember more." He blinked hastily and shrugged, shifting in his seat. "I know she loved me," he said. "I only wish . . ."

"You wish you remembered her loving you," I said. "Instead of simply knowing it." He nodded and promptly busied himself with his own sandwich.

It was a dodge—one his mother never would have made. Perhaps he took after me in some ways, after so many centuries. But I, too, yearned for a subject change. "Could I ask for your technical expertise?"

Ruthie nodded, wiping a droplet of au jus from the corner of his mouth.

"Could someone alter a skimmer to erase someone's memories?"

"Theoretically yes," he said, somewhat muffled, then chewed a bit and thought a bit and swallowed. "The skimmers use the same kind of light we use to record memory-books in the Library—and all the bodies on the *Fairweather* are particularly sensitive to that kind of light. The molecular markers, you see."

"How precise is it?"

"Not very, I expect—you wouldn't be able to choose your targets. The most you could do would be to erase whatever memory the person was trying to project. Might take several attempts. Would be dangerous, too, for the person you're working on." He picked at the crusts of his prime rib dip. "Skimmers aren't as powerful as anything in the Library, but they're still nothing to go fooling around with."

"Could you induce a stroke by trying to erase a memory?"

"I should bloody well think so— Hang on, this is about Flora, isn't it? That's how she died, do you think?"

I grimaced but nodded.

Violet was going to be disappointed if it turned out this opposite-of-a-murder involved something that looked an awful lot like murder.

A shame—it had seemed such a pleasant, wholesome case at first.

BETWEEN THE ANTIKYTHERA Club visit and the times we'd had to move Peregrine around the ship, rumors about the baby's existence were flooding the *Fairweather*'s public communication channels. I was keeping abreast of some of the more ludicrous conspiracy theories—particularly the one that said Medical's retromats had broken down and we were all going to have to be babies again if we wanted new bodies—so I managed to catch the moment when the Board's official announcement came through, essentially unchanged from the draft I'd sent them. And with my name appended in case passengers had further questions.

All hell, in textual form, broke loose.

I spent the following hour in the Antikythera bar. Ruthie took the baby after lunch and John continued his shift, pouring memory cocktails for club members and casting anxious glances my way. I typed replies to alarmed friends and broadcast calming, repetitive statements from my pocket watch until my finger bones ached, taking only occasional breaks to listen to two mathematicians debate the geometry of compression at beyond light speeds, or some such thing. It was a relief to bathe briefly in a river of words that I didn't understand and wasn't required to respond to.

Then, with a wealth of dread, I returned to my office in the Bureau, where I was sure people were waiting to speak to me in person rather than by note.

My dread proved thoroughly justified when Jason Ipcar turned up. Leloup savoringly knocked on my office door to inform me of the arrival, before retreating to the Jason-free serenity of his own office.

The scenario writer stood up from the ochre sofa when I opened the door to the waiting room. He looked me up, looked me down, and let his lip curl with disdain. "You Dorothy Gentleman?" he asked without preamble.

"That's correct, Mr. Ipcar," I said. I had only spent three seconds in this man's company and already I wished Flora could have dumped him a thousand times. Out of an air lock, for preference. He was handsome enough, as men went, but the mulish set of that chiseled jaw and the cold gleam in those limpid eyes proclaimed him a nasty, selfish piece of work.

"I want my child, Miss Gentleman," he said. "And I've come to claim him."

I smiled. I'd been looking for a suspect for the kidnapping—someone either desperate or foolish enough to have attempted to take Peregrine by force. Jason Ipcar had all but served himself up to me on a platter.

Oh, this was going to be fun. I'd had to watch my words all day around sensitive, subtle, and anxious people. But now Fate had handed me a prime fish to fillet with the sharpest side of my tongue—and I couldn't wait.

I beckoned him inside. "Why don't we step into my office?"

He made for the chair behind my desk—the nerve!—and only a pointed cough from me diverted him onto the sofa instead.

I didn't sit. I merely leaned a hip against the desk and folded my arms at him. "Have you had children before, Mr. Ipcar?"

He snorted. "Not any I'm aware of."

It took a particular brand of effrontery to make that joke so many centuries after it had become irrelevant. My helpful smile didn't waver. "May I ask what makes you interested in gaining custody of this baby at this time?"

"I believe in protecting what's mine," he replied.

"And you believe the baby is yours?"

"Flora and I have been together almost a year now. I'm aware there were others during that time—for me as well as for her, mind—"

"I'm sure," I muttered.

"—but the odds point to me being the father. And I won't sit back while others take advantage of my child. He's my responsibility, mine."

Here we approached a motive for a kidnapping, if he'd done it. "What kind of advantage concerns you?"

He shifted in his seat. "You've seen how many wild rumors there are about this baby—how it happened, what it means, whose it is. We haven't had this kind of sensation in decades on the *Fairweather*. And I know more than one writer—playwrights, journalists, scenesters like myself—who are already cobbling together a treatment of the story. Someone is going to make a lot of money off this baby." He clapped one hand on his knee and leaned forward, elbow akimbo. "Someone needs to see that the baby gets his rightful share. As the source of the story."

And the rights holder. Which, of course, Peregrine's guardian would be until Peregrine himself came of age. It wasn't a system we had much experience with on board ship—our passengers had all been of legal age for centuries—but it featured in enough of the flickers and stage shows that everyone thought they knew how it worked. Like the basket with the significant fabric, or the maid who's secretly the heir.

Jason Ipcar, in short, was here because he thought there would be fame. Money was easy to come by on the

Fairweather—but reputation, popularity, and attention were in comparatively short supply. Reason enough to attempt a kidnapping, particularly if he thought the child was his by rights. It was extremely stupid, of course, because as soon as he produced the baby and made his claim, any ship's detective would be able to say *Oh look, here is our kidnapper.* He was lucky Leloup wasn't on the case: My colleague liked things tidy, and this was as tidy as it came.

"I'm so glad to hear you have the baby's best interests at heart," I lied through my smiling teeth, keeping my voice soft and my eyes softer. "We've already seen one attempt on the child's safety, last night. A shame you were not there to protect him."

"Well, I didn't know about him, did I? I had . . . other obligations last night."

"I'm sure a man like you must have," I murmured. "Anywhere in particular?"

"The Sofia was premiering one of my latest scripts. A few of us adjourned to the Rococo afterward to celebrate."

Ah, the Rococo, one of the ship's longest-established cocktail palaces. Infamous for their debauchery and shameless rumormongering: If Ipcar had been there, a dozen bartenders and waitstaff would happily confirm.

Odds were, then, that he was not our kidnapper.

But I could still justify tormenting him a little, to relieve my own feelings and frighten him out of meddling further in a case he had no business in. "Considering the interest in the child," I began, "I'm sure you'll understand that both the Board and the Bureau are eager to stay informed and involved." I let my smile widen a little. "Very involved. Particularly since this would be your first child. We are fiercely interested in providing an immense amount of support to this baby's parent."

"What kind of support?" he inquired suspiciously.

"Well." I let the syllable unroll like a carpet, and then I launched in. "Of course there is the full background inquiry, home examination, and thorough interviews with references you may offer as to your character and behavior—not a problem for a man of your caliber, I am sure."

Poor Jason was looking a trifle green around the gills. "All that?"

"That's the preliminaries," I chirped. "As well as, it hardly needs mentioning, the educational component."

"He's hardly old enough for schooling yet, surely?" He tugged anxiously at the knot on his tie.

"Not for him, Mr. Ipcar. For you." His jaw dropped. "Of course we'll have to teach you about infant care, speech development, environmental enrichment, the importance of a consistent routine, sleep training, nutrition, and emergency aid. I mean," I said, "you did say you intended to be a responsible guardian?" He gave a nod, a bare, anxious jerk of his chin. "So then you'll have no trouble with the weekly check-up visits, either. Just to make sure the child's home is comfortable and hygienic."

Every word seemed to be a new pin, deflating his paternal enthusiasm. "You might pay for a professional cleaner," he put in. He was trying, but he was wavering.

"Oh, we wouldn't dream of being so officious," I purred. "We will of course be setting up a trust for the child, along with any royalties due him for adaptations of his story, which monies will be his when he reaches legal age. And not a second before." I lowered my voice, as if imparting a great secret. "You may rest assured we will guard his trust with everything the Board can bring to bear, Mr. Ipcar. Many of us on board and on the Board are parents, grandparents, relatives, teachers, and guardians. We have not had a child to protect in several centuries, but we do not intend to let that make us less than fully diligent in our responsibilities."

"So I see." His glance had begun flicking to either side, as if he were an animal trapped and looking for escape. "So I. So—when? Listen, Miss Gentleman, if I could just ask you a few—"

I raised a hand. "Mr. Ipcar." He froze, mouth still open around the syllables of a word I didn't need or want to hear. "Let me set your mind at ease. You have no child."

"But—but . . ." He slumped back, wanting but not daring to believe me. "But Flora and I—"

"The baby is not yours. You have no strong claim to custody, any more than any other ordinary passenger—though of course you may petition for it if you wish."

"No!" he squeaked, and cleared his throat. "No," he said. "But if it's not mine—then whose is it?"

"The father has been informed and is taking the steps he feels are appropriate," I said. "That is all I can say at this time. But rest assured that the child will be well cared for—"

"Good, good," he said, and shot up from the sofa as though gravity had briefly ceased to restrain him. "I appreciate the Board taking on this Herculean task, and trust that—as a disinterested outsider—"

"Goodbye, Mr. Ipcar," I said, merciful as a hanging judge, and the man saw his chance and all but fled the Bureau.

It didn't bring me any closer to our kidnapper, but I felt heaps more cheerful about the case all the same.

***

I SENT A note to Melodie Chee at the Rococo—a delightful woman, an absolute gem of a cocktail mixer—to confirm Mr. Ipcar's alibi, and gathered my things. The solar lights were beginning to shade into twilight's lavender; it had been a long, exhausting day, and I was grateful for it to be over.

When I made my way home, every inch of my soul

bruised from too many kinds of pettiness—as though I'd been trampled by the feet of a million furious ants—it was only to find an official summons from the Board. They were demanding a hearing on what they were calling the Infant Incident, and they wanted it two days from now in the Star Chamber. With witnesses.

Most of the time a detective could simply submit their report in paper form and never hear a thing about it again. Truth found, questions answered, wrapped up neatly with a bow and put away in a box somewhere like a grandparent's love letters. Occasionally one of us unearthed the kind of iniquity that required convening the Crime Committee for a trial, which was a long drawn-out process that moved very slowly and in which everyone spoke very carefully through a phalanx of legal representatives.

This was neither of those things: A hearing was called when there came an event whose mystery the Board felt they needed to understand, and whose complexity they wanted me to answer for firsthand. Perhaps a trial would come later—certainly I had been planning to recommend one in my full write-up of the case—but at present the Board wanted to be able to ask questions and receive answers and feel as though they were doing their duty as governors of the ship and its passengers.

I generally approved of meddling and nosiness—except, of course, when it was turned against me. Alas, answering to the Board was a part of the job, and I could see little use in fighting it.

I whipped up a hasty dinner for myself from the autochef and began laying out the facts of the case. Timelines, names of witnesses, loose ends still in need of tying, and, for that last one, a lengthy dive into some very specific, uncommon databases. John and Ruthie's custody petition, too, since this would be my best opportunity of seeing that addressed with due speed. Otherwise that kind of paperwork could take a year or more.

Hours later, swimming in text, my head snapped up as someone knocked softly on my door.

A flash of panic, hastily tamped down. A kidnapper was not, I told myself, likely to knock before entering. And anyway the baby wasn't here.

I rubbed the crust from my eyes and opened the door—only to find Violet St. Owen there on the threshold, looking like all my weaknesses made flesh. Her hair was up, her smile was shy, and the solar-lamp evening made her skin glow gold. She was wearing a blue knit dress she'd no doubt made herself, festooned with bobbles, and it looked so soft and touchable it made me want to throw myself into her arms and weep. "I came to see how your baby blanket was coming along," she said, and then—stars help me—dimpled. "But I suppose you haven't had much in the way of knitting time today."

"Come in and have a drink," I said, stepping back and yielding to the inevitable. "I'll tell you all about it."

Sexual temptations were easy to resist—it felt noble somehow to lust and pine in romantic silence. But I'd been buffeted by a thousand passengers' very loud fears and nightmares for the past several hours, as I defended the well-being of a tiny human who had no idea what kind of chaos he'd accidentally set off by merely being brought into the world. I was in desperate need of some kindness and a listening ear.

I couldn't trust Violet in everything, but I could trust her for this.

I went to the autochef for drinks while Violet pulled a spare chair up to the table. The surface was littered with my notes and outlines, not to mention the forms I'd been filling in to officially notify the people I was calling as witnesses. It was a dismaying amount of paper, white and suffocating as a snowbank.

Violet clearly thought so, too, frowning as she nudged things just enough to make room for the glass I brought her: a double pour of starlight sparkling on the ocean. "Is the case going well or not? I can't tell by looking."

"Put it this way," I said, sitting down hard and taking a long pull of mostly gin with a hint of winter's first snow. "I'm almost at the part where I seriously consider putting out my own eyes with a pair of fountain pens."

Violet raised her glass in a sardonic toast. "Paperwork seems a shabby reward for the preservation of law and order."

"Paperwork *is* law and order," I countered. "The papers are what make us a society and not just a gaggle of desperate people sharing a geography. We set up a system because a system can be permanent, where human beings are not."

Violet's mouth flattened. "You're presuming the system is supposed to serve the people, rather than the people serving the system."

"It is."

"It is, if you're thinking like a good person. Trouble is, when you tell people the system is good because it's different than people, some people hear: *The system is more important than people.* And then they act accordingly. And someone who doesn't deserve it gets hurt."

"You're not wrong," I sighed, thinking of Leloup. "Here's the main thrust: I am trying to find a paperwork way to say that this baby deserves to be classified as a passenger, no different than the rest of us."

Violet nodded. "And the bulk of the law is standing in your way?"

"Not the bulk," I protested, then slumped a little. "About a half-bulk," I admitted. "Maybe two-thirds." I explained the bind I was in, where there was no current process for designating someone as a passenger. Using planetary law would almost certainly get Peregrine an official identity, and swiftly, but he'd only have the one lifetime available to him and would never actually see the planet whose laws governed his existence. "So either he belongs to the planet he never sets foot on, or he's designated an automaton or a pet or a—a piece of luggage," I finished. "And either way, he won't be granted a memory-book. It feels like sentencing him to death. I cannot permit that to happen, but I can't see how to prevent it."

Violet was silent a long while, long fingers tapping on the side of her highball glass. "I think you might be too focused on the process," she said at last.

"What do you mean?"

She smiled. "How much of that baby blanket do you have done?"

I brought over my knitting and showed her my few scant rows. Barely more than a border, at this point, and only a hint of the gradient I was building.

Violet took the baby blanket carefully, slipped the needle out of the loops, and gave the working yarn a confident pull. An entire row unraveled beneath my horrified eyes. "Steady on!" I said.

"Oh, as if you've never frogged a project before," she said. "Now look." She held up the unraveled working yarn, which was not smooth and silky like the rest of the skein. No, it zigged and zagged back and forth from where I'd knitted with it. "The yarn carries the memory of how it was handled," Violet said. "You can pull out all the stitches, but you can't erase the experience. It's a part of the material now. Just like the baby is a part of the *Fairweather*'s society, no matter what the paperwork says about it."

I was still staring at that kinky bit of wool. "You're saying the yarn remembers."

"I'm saying Peregrine *is* a passenger. He's on this ship, the same as the rest of us. That is a plain fact. So instead of trying to unlock the law with cleverness as if it were a puzzle box, or a riddle set by a wizard in a fairy tale, go right to the heart of the question and ask yourself: What does any passenger *deserve*?"

"The yarn remembers," I repeated, and began to laugh.

Violet peered at me, her bright eyes puzzled. "Just how strong was that drink?" she murmured.

"Just strong enough," I replied—and impulsively grabbed her hand, raising it to my lips. "Thank you," I said. "You've given me a wonderful idea about how to turn the law against itself."

"Well, it's not crime," Violet replied, blushing, "but I suppose if it's the best you can do."

* * *

MY STOMACH WAS fluttering, my hands were clammy, and I was in my sharpest-tailored suit. Sweat had already begun to gather at the small of my back, and I would have to be careful not to lock my knees lest I pass out in front of the Board and all my witnesses.

There were five minutes to go until the hearing started, and I was still waiting on my most important piece of evidence. Baxenden had promised to bring it as promptly as he could, but until then I could only pace beside my podium and fret.

Calling this room the Star Chamber had been someone's idea of wit. There was a dais at one round end, on which the Board took seats behind a long length of scarred and polished wood. Not retromatted, I recalled—they'd installed this before leaving Earth. Something about remembering our roots, branching out onto other worlds, the usual kind of overwrought symbolism that public institutions were so fond of.

They called this room the Star Chamber because it was open to the stars.

Or looked it, anyway: The round walls were carved out with arches of diamond-glass that peered out onto the sparkles and streaks of space. Grand windows curved into a dome above as well, with delicate tracery like the stone of an ancient cathedral. It was meant to remind us to be humble, I suppose, but it only really left me feeling cold and exposed beneath all that space.

Or maybe that was the way the Board was radiating pedantic bureaucratic displeasure. As though I'd arranged for an entire baby to be created in secret just to ruin their Thursday afternoon.

Behind me were the bench seats where witnesses waited to give testimony. Flora and Anne were clutching each other's hands, Norris was sitting beside his mother looking cool but tense, Hugh Renois was a little bit apart with a dark suit and a vest that was nearly blinding in its plaid intensity. Ruthie and John had Peregrine in his basket between them; my nephew caught me watching and gave a jaunty little wave.

At last—at long last!—with only a minute to spare, Baxenden slipped in with a carrying case in his hand, and sent me a thumbs-up indicating success.

I gave myself sixty seconds to simply focus on breathing in and out, hoping it would calm my galloping heart.

All too quickly, the current Chair of the Board gaveled the meeting to order and gestured at me to begin.

A hearing was a little bit like a stage play, or perhaps a magic trick, and as I wiped the clamminess from my palms and walked to the podium facing the Board, I had a moment to wish for some of Anne Godfrey's ability to set the scene and color it persuasively.

But I was only a detective, not an artist. I'd have to hope the truth didn't need too much dressing up.

"Members of the Board," I began, "thank you for coming. This is my full report on the passenger currently known as Peregrine, who was born five months ago but who only came to my attention this week. The baby was created in the traditional manner..."

And we were off.

The first bit was straightforward enough: Both Flora and Hugh Renois had visited Medical for examinations, and I had both reports in my hand explaining that the fertility limits we implemented on all bodies had reversed themselves in what seemed to be random chance. If the couple had never crossed paths with each other, we'd never have known anything about it. "It's possible this is more frequent than we realize," I said, "so I've asked the *Fairweather* to add this to the list of things we check for during a passenger's annual physical."

"Have the controls been reinstituted?" one Board member demanded from beneath a bristling mustache.

"We have made the request," I said, preserving the parents' medical privacy.

He harrumphed but didn't press further.

"When she found out she was pregnant, Flora Tilburn surprised herself and decided to keep the baby," I went on. "She stopped updating her memory-book—not wanting the ship to learn of the child's existence—and moved out into an apartment on Forward Port Six. She gave birth alone."

One of the Board members made a horrified sound.

"She maintained a correspondence with her former roommate, Mrs. Anne Godfrey, and at one point visited a man she erroneously believed to be the father. But most of her days were spent with her son, whom she called Florian—and because she loved the flickers and wanted to share them, she asked her friend's son, Norris Godfrey, to build her a skimmer of her own.

"This, it turned out, is what killed her."

Behind me, Anne gasped.

I turned to see Flora's cheeks had gone pale, and her knuckles were white where her hand clutched Anne's.

I softened my expression but not my volume, wishing I could have presented this next fact to her more privately. But I couldn't risk it getting out before the hearing. "Flora Tilburn spent hours every day using a skimmer that had been altered to slowly wipe away any memory she tried to project. She believed she needed more practice as a projectionist, because the images seemed cloudy and vague to her. But the more she focused on those memories, the vaguer they got. Until they started to vanish altogether. One by one, piece by piece, her memories—the very stuff of her life—were chipped away. Eventually the strain was too great, and she suffered a fatal stroke while out one day in a clothing shop. She was reembodied, but it had been five months since she updated her memory-book. Her memories of her son were gone." I reached into the podium and pulled out Flora's diary in its blue cloth cover, and set it on the evidence table before me. "At the time of her death, she was keeping a physical diary. Her early entries are detailed and specific, but later ones are baffled and confused. She knew something was wrong—but she didn't know she'd been so deeply betrayed by a friend."

"Who?" Anne demanded.

"Yes, who?" asked the Chair.

"Norris Godfrey," I replied. "I call him now for questioning."

Heads swiveled to look at him.

Norris didn't look at all surprised, only resigned, as he walked forward and took a seat in the broad wooden witness chair. His cool face chilled further at the faces turned his way. Then he sneered at Peregrine, of all people, fussing innocently in my nephew's protective arms. "I suppose he's already told you everything."

"My nephew?" I asked.

"The *baby*."

We all looked at the infant, and then back at Norris. But the man seemed to be serious. "Of course he has," I said, papering over my astonishment with pure, artificial confidence. "But we will require you to fill in the gaps anyway, Mr. Godfrey. What did you have against Flora?"

"Absolutely nothing," he said.

"And yet you tried to erase all her memories of your mother."

"I had to," he said, and that sneer returned in full force. It was an ugly expression, the kind that no amount of physical beauty could overcome. Hugh Renois's nose wrinkled to see it, and Flora actually flinched away. "Just because she meant no harm doesn't mean no harm was done. She is a flighty, frivolous soul who only lives for flighty, frivolous entertainment. Absolutely nothing wrong with that—until she pulled my poor, vulnerable mother into her orbit."

I thought of Flora's diary, which had almost as much of Anne in it as Flora. "How did they meet?"

"In Medical, after a reembodiment. They started taking walks together, and Flora invited her to a matinee. Then it was shows every evening, and let's move in together, and five years ago they actually started the Palace to show flickers of their own devising." His hands on the wooden railing were clenched tight, nails biting into the ancient wood. "And suddenly she had no room in her schedule for her son—her own flesh and blood. If I hadn't been a skimmer technician, I might have never seen her at all. But Flora thought she was blossoming," he spat. "She thought my mother was finally starting to *live*."

"You said I had a point," Flora put in.

"Because I knew if I fought with you, I would lose my mother completely," he said, whirling to glare at her. "And then you found out you were having a child. A replacement for me, whom you would have let my mother help raise—until I convinced you, using your own selfish words, that she deserved her freedom."

Flora flushed with the urge to argue, but subsided when Anne pressed her hand.

"Was that when you worked out how to erase Flora's memories?" I asked.

"Erasing memories was never my intention," Norris protested. "I was *trying* to discover a way to *transmit* memories. To carry them whole from the projectionist into the viewer. The substance, not merely the reflection." He turned to look at Anne, and his eyes softened. "So that I would not be dependent upon my mother for the memories of my father."

"I did the best I could," Anne said sadly. "I showed you everything I remembered."

"You did," Norris said. "And then you stopped. You had better things to do. You forgot that without you, I could never see my father's face at all."

"It's been three hundred years!"

"Oh, is that all?" he scoffed. "Three centuries and you stop being a mother. How long, I wonder, could you manage to stay a friend?" He glared down at where Flora's hand entwined with Anne's.

His mother only tightened her grip. Her face was sad but stoic. "How did you manage to hide this resentment from me for so long?"

"It's easy to hide things from someone who isn't looking," he said cuttingly.

"So when Flora moved out," I slid in, picking up the thread, "you saw an opportunity. You couldn't steal your mother's memories like you wanted—"

"It is not theft to want what's mine by right!"

"—so you decided instead to take away the woman she loved."

Norris looked at Flora, not unkindly. "You couldn't put her first, now that you had a child to care for—he deserved to be your first priority. You weren't meant to die. You were only meant to forget."

"But she did die," I said. "The way you altered the skimmer is very hard on the human mind, I'm told. Just because you meant no harm doesn't mean no harm was done."

Norris waved a dismissive hand. "You don't know anything about it. You said yourself you barely even go to the flickers."

"I've learned a great deal since then," I said. "And besides, we have the skimmer right here."

I signaled Baxenden, who stepped forward. The case

he carried was opened, and within it was the now-familiar shape: a flat-brimmed hat, a lens, and a light.

Norris was staring at it like it was a viper. "That's not possible," he said. "I destroyed it, I know I did."

"You sent it to the reclamation center, yes," I replied. "But did you know: Everything that the reclamation center destroys, the *Fairweather* first makes a record of? A perfect scan, down to the last molecule. Civilians can't access these plans—but detectives can. And we can replicate them." I put a hand on the flat metal edge. "Members of the Board, Mr. Godfrey's altered skimmer is as much a blunt instrument as a hammer, or a brick, or a stone. Used repeatedly, it breaks down entire chains of recollection, until what's left is fragile as a cobweb. Flora was using this for at least three months—until she collapsed. She was reembodied and her memories restored from the Library, which dated to before the birth of her son. To her, it was as if he never existed."

"So the baby was left alone?" a Board member asked.

"Of course not," I replied. "Flora was a careful, caring mother, as her diary from those months proves. She would never leave her child alone, not even for a simple errand. She left him with Mr. Godfrey." I smiled. "And I can prove it. Or rather—Mr. Godfrey can."

Everyone stared at the witness, who could only stare back. I stepped away and wheeled out a small screen as Baxenden stepped forward, along with Gaskill, who'd come to be a show of strength at my request. Gaskill clamped one hand on each of Norris's shoulders, and Baxenden lifted the skimmer toward Norris's head.

His eyes shot wide when he realized what we meant to do. "No!" he cried. "Please!"

But Baxenden was ruthless. I'd insisted on it. Gaskill held tight as Baxenden fixed the brim in place and pressed the switch to begin projecting. A jumble of light and color flashed onto the screen, a kaleidoscope of ghosts and images and rooms.

"Show us the last time Flora saw her son," I said.

Norris clamped his mouth and eyes mulishly shut, but the skimmer did its job against his will: The images coalesced into a view of the apartment in Forward Port Six. Flora, pale and shaky, handing her son over to Norris and then walking out the door. Norris began playing with the child, the baby silently laughing in delight, until the real Norris began to get control back and the image started to fray.

"Now show us two days ago, when you tried to kidnap him," I said.

Norris shook his head sharply in refusal—but it was like those word games where someone tells you not to think of green elephants. The memory obeys, even as the will objects. We watched—all of us, witnesses and detectives and Board members—as Norris expertly wiped the lock on an apartment door and crept in the dark toward Ruthie and

Peregrine, blissfully asleep. My nephew's whisper of "Crimes Committed!" mercifully went unmarked by anyone except John and myself.

Norris's memories faded again, and I continued my explanation. "When Flora was brought to Medical, she stopped responding to Anne Godfrey's notes. Anne grew concerned, and after a full day had passed she went in search of Flora's new apartment, despite all Flora's warnings to keep away. She found the apartment and found the baby, on his own." I turned to our witness, sagging on the stand. "I assume you had been called away on official business of some kind?"

Norris was now a beaten man, visibly nauseous and yearning for the end. "I was planning on coming back," he said. "It's not like the child was going to walk away on his own."

"Not as such, no," I said. "But Anne found him, and believed Flora had been turned back into a baby—she had been projecting a film called *The Follies of Youth*, and—"

"Yes, we've all seen it," the Chair interrupted.

"We had a private screening for the Board last week," the member on the end confirmed, with a little nod to Anne. "Most entertaining."

"Oh," I said. "Oh, that's—that's—well." I cleared my throat and pressed onward. "Anne conveyed the baby to my nephew, Mr. Rutherford Talmadge IV, who brought the child to my attention. We determined parentage and unraveled the chain of events that led to the child's creation. I recommend the Crime Committee be convened to charge Mr. Godfrey with manslaughter, or at the very least with reckless endangerment."

I nodded at Baxenden, who removed the skimmer. Norris's eyes glistened with tears of horror, his face mottled with dread and rage. "You fiendish woman," he hissed. "You could have killed me!"

"With that?" I waved at the skimmer. "Unlikely. That's the Palace's skimmer, which you repaired with your own hands. Perfectly safe, since you weren't trying to erase any of your mother's memories. Quite the opposite, in fact." As Norris gaped, I only smiled, permitting myself a tiny flash of well-earned smugness. "I'm afraid I had to mislead you a little, in the interest of getting you to show us the truth."

"Excuse me, Miss Gentleman." A Board member broke in, over Norris's wordless outraged sounds. "One more question. Why did Mr. Godfrey attempt to kidnap the child?"

"Didn't I mention?" I said. "He thought the baby was a witness."

Everyone looked at Peregrine, who had his hand in his mouth up to the wrist.

"Really?" the Chair asked, dripping with skepticism.

"It was the first thing he said on the witness stand. I quote: 'I suppose he's already told you everything.'"

Norris's mouth went slack. "You said he had!"

"He cannot yet speak," I said. "How would he have told us anything?"

"The skimmer!" Norris sputtered. "Obviously!"

"Well, that is an intriguing thought," I said with a grin. "Shall we try it?"

Norris was moved aside by Gaskill, and Ruthie brought Peregrine forward to the witness chair. The skimmer tottered a little on his small head until Ruthie steadied it with one hand. "There's a good little man," he murmured, amused.

I stepped forward and crouched, so my face was level with Peregrine's and his eyes fixed on me. "Hullo, little one," I said, low and soft and fond.

His face creased into a smile.

I couldn't see what happened on the screen behind me, but there was a general gasp of astonishment. It fizzed in my veins like applause.

I whispered a few more things to Peregrine, then stood up and turned back to the board. "My nephew has been caring for the child the past few days," I said, and waved Ruthie in front.

My nephew's eyes widened and his cheek paled a little, but his lip refused to quiver as he stepped around and beamed down at Peregrine. "Your hat's at quite a rakish angle, little man," he said, crouching down as I had. "What will the society papers think?" Peregrine chortled as Ruthie tweaked his nose, and waved his hands imperiously.

And this time I could see what the baby was unwittingly projecting. Ruthie's face was up there—weirdly proportioned and rippling like a sheet on a clothesline, but recognizable all the same. It had a kind of shimmer to it, a swirl of color that bubbled up and out, and it kept melting into other expressions. The color of Ruthie's tie changed abruptly, and I realized it was switching between the one he wore today and the one he'd worn yesterday at the Antikythera Club.

"And now," I said, "let's see what his mother's face shows us." And I beckoned Flora up to the front of the room.

She was anxious, I could see, but she trusted me enough to come forward. Ruthie stepped back behind Peregrine as Flora slowly bent to look at her son close up. "Hello there," she whispered.

The images exploded.

Bright colors, painfully vivid. Flora's face but slightly older, with a slightly different nose and a different cut to her hair. Flora laughing, Flora in darkness, Flora reaching out for an embrace.

The real Flora turned and stared at her own reflection, at the love she no longer remembered so evident in her face.

Surprisingly, it was Ruthie who spoke next. "You said he was too young to form memories," he said. He looked a little heartbroken watching Flora and Peregrine, and no wonder.

"He makes them," I replied. "He just doesn't keep them. Not for more than a few weeks, anyway. As he gets older his brain will start holding on to things longer and longer." I turned back to the Board. "I recommend we begin archiving Peregrine in the Library when he turns one, and every three months or so after that."

"Hang on," said the Chair. "We haven't even begun to address the question of the child's status yet."

"Well, we'd better do it quick," I said. "The Charter holds equality of access to the Library and Medical as one of our founding principles. We have the right to be archived, and the right to reembodiment. The older this child gets, the more galling it's going to be that he isn't permitted to preserve himself the way the rest of us are."

"Do we really want to reward this kind of behavior, though?" the mustached Board member sputtered.

"His parents did not conceive him on purpose, and couldn't have if they tried," I argued. "If you prefer, think of it not as a reward, but as imposing an obligation: He is *required* to update his memory-book every three months. This requirement also demands he be reembodied, so as to continue updating his memories. Without your help, he will die in thirty, fifty, seventy-five years or so." I felt my mouth quirk. "You, as the Board, could sentence him to life."

A hum went across the dais, as Board members turned

to mutter to one another. "And his mother would be raising him?"

"Not necessarily," I said, keeping my voice level, though I wanted to shout with the joy of almost-triumph. "Rutherford Talmadge IV and John Pengelly have applied for custody. The paperwork is only waiting on your approval."

Flora looked up at Ruthie, relief stark on her face. "You would be taking care of him?"

Ruthie nodded, swallowing hard.

Flora stood, her knees only a little wobbly. "Could—could I come visit, from time to time?"

Ruthie smiled even as tears sprang to his eyes. "I would like that."

Flora spun on her heel to glare at the Board. "As his mother, I support Mr. Talmadge's custody petition."

"As does his father," said Hugh Renois, rising to his feet in the audience.

"Any opposition?" The Chair looked at the audience and then to his fellow Board members, who performed a series of shrugs, scowls, and shakings of the head. "Very well. Custodial petition is approved."

Four parental faces lit up with separate flavors of relief.

"And the memory-book?"

The Chair waved a hand. "Yes, yes, Miss Gentleman, you've made your point. He shall have full rights to memory storage and reembodiment. After all," he said, with a glance around the dais, "do we want to be known as the Board who killed the first new human child for three hundred years?"

Clearly this line of logic was a new one, as many Board members' eyes went wide to hear it. Even the member with the mustache looked a bit cowed as he considered how such a decision would look to next year's voters.

Ah, democracy.

"Any other questions?" the Chair demanded, and banged the gavel when no one spoke up. "Then let us convene the Crime Committee, and consider this hearing complete."

The room immediately buzzed with sound as everyone began talking at once. Gaskill and Baxenden led Norris away to be placed under house arrest—and possible guard, considering the man's way with a lock—and Anne ran forward to embrace Flora.

Ruthie removed the skimmer and gathered his son up into his arms.

I moved forward, buoyant with success. "So it seems now I'm a great-aunt," I said, ruffling my fingers through Peregrine's silk-soft curls.

"You've always been great to me," Ruthie replied.

I winced. "Good heavens, I'm far too sober for that kind of punnery. Shame on you, Rutherford." I gave the infant one more pat. "You're going to have to start setting a better example from now on."

For the first time since this whole escapade started, Ruthie looked down at Peregrine with alarm—not for the baby, but for himself. "Oh no, do you think so?"

I laughed. "Don't worry," I said, glancing to where John had formed a little group with Flora and Anne and Hugh. "You'll have plenty of help."

THE NEWS WENT out all over the public channels, and I spent the rest of the day in the Bureau answering official queries and putting out statements and even, flatteringly, giving a brief interview to a journalist whose questions were almost embarrassingly complimentary.

And then the triumph ebbed and there was only me, alone. Quiet and drained and a little restless, as I always found myself at the end of a case.

Naturally, I ended up at Violet St. Owen's yarn shop.

I'd deliberately left it late, so this time it was I who approached her with the golden solar sunset all around me in the ten minutes before she was scheduled to close. "I've brought a pattern for you," I said. "To thank you for your help."

And I set the skimmer plans down on the glass counter.

Not without a qualm or two, mind. It wasn't every day

I broke the law, and my constitution was threatening to rebel. I had to wipe my damp palms against my trouser legs as Violet unrolled the schematics and raised an interested eyebrow. "Are these the ones Norris Godfrey altered?" she asked.

"They are," I said.

Her eyes met mine, shrewd and surprised in equal measure. "Are you supposed to be giving these to ordinary passengers?"

"Absolutely not," I said. "But today I had to go and argue nineteen grown adults into not letting an infant die out of sheer apathy—so my sympathy with the lawmakers is at its very lowest ebb."

She leaned forward over the counter, on her elbows. Her hands were very near mine—almost but not quite touching. My skin buzzed with the proximity. "You're not afraid of what I'll do with these?"

"No more than I'm afraid of my fellow detectives," I said, and thought of Leloup. "Less than some, in fact."

Violet smiled. The plans were whisked into a drawer of the counter and locked away with a key she kept on a necklace around her neck. "I'll put them somewhere safer tomorrow," she said. "For tonight . . ." She cocked her head, golden hair tumbling over one shoulder and gleaming almost as bright as her smile. "I wonder if I might buy a ship's detective a drink."

"At the Antikythera Club?" I suggested. "I've just gotten word my membership application's been approved." High-profile hearings could be good for the social status, it seemed.

Violet shook her head. "Congratulations—but perhaps another time," she said. "I've got somewhere far more intimate in mind."

"Suits me," I said. She dimmed the lights and locked the door—and for the first time, I let go of the law, and took her hand.

ACKNOWLEDGMENTS

Books are not children—ask any T-ball coach which one they'd prefer at the plate—but one thing books and children have in common is that they're better when their creators have help. I give thanks to my agent, the inimitable Courtney Miller-Callihan, for the warmth of her wisdom and insight; to my editor, Mara Delgado-Sanchez, for quickness and unerring precision; to artist Marcos Chin and designer Shreya Gupta for the exquisite beauty of the cover; to Caro Perny and Julia Bergen for tireless enthusiasm in publicity and marketing.

And of course, to my own nephews B and O, distant but never forgotten. I love you both, even when you outgrow the sweaters.

ABOUT THE AUTHOR

OLIVIA WAITE writes queer science fiction, fantasy, historical romance, and essays. She is the romance fiction columnist for the *New York Times Book Review*.